Katrina's Diary

RON LEATH

ISBN:
ISBN-13: 978-1-7330629-2-3
ISBN-10: 1713062920

DEDICATION

To my amazing wife, Ebone. My wonderful kids, Jahiara and Tahraun. I do this for you. I love you. Thank you for being there for me.

TABLE OF CONTENTS

ACKNOWLEDGMENTS

Wow, a whole series completed in less than a year! I would've never had this dream come true if it wasn't for a few people. First, I thank God above for giving me this skill. Next, my wife Ebone for sharing her thoughts. And everyone who has been down since day one. You know who you are! You believed in me. Thank you all!

Katrina's Diary

Sometimes, I sit and wonder if my life would have turned out any different had I not made some of those foolish ass decisions. Better yet, I wonder if I would've been any different had both of my parents been in my life; like so many other kids I saw growing up. Shit… probably not. I can't make excuses for the shit I've done. I just have to accept it and keep it moving.

I grew up in Los Angeles. Not the Hollywood shit you see on TV—I'm from the hood, where every day is a fight for survival. When they say, trust no one, take that shit to the heart. I've been fucked over so many times, and that's why I only have one friend; my homegirl, Toya. My mom is dead, and my pops hasn't been around since who knows when. I do have a big brother, but he's just as fucked up as I am. Better yet, that nigga is ten times worse than I could ever be.

Maybe one day things will change. I damn sure hope so. But moving forward, I want to document my life with a diary. Since I feel alone in this world, maybe writing will help me get by.

While I'm thankful to still be alive, I still have visions of dying at an early age. If I do die young, I want people to not only see my struggles, but also my come up. This is my story written by me, so can't another muthafucka tell lies about me.

Goodnight

Katrina J.

Introduction

There was a loud knock on my room door. You know those loud, consistent knocks. I was in the middle of a good ass dream. Hell, the knock disturbed me so much, by the time I opened my eyes, I had forgotten what my dream was about.

"Who is it?" I screamed, as if it was anyone else besides my brother, Nate. We were the only ones living there, but I had to say something to let him know that I didn't feel like being bothered. I always kept my room door locked and he still tried to get in.

"Trina, open up. I gotta holla at you before I go to work."

I drilled my head into the pillow and stayed there for a few seconds before finally getting up. I then opened the door for his annoying ass and laid back down. "What do you want, Nate?" I asked. I checked my phone and read through some of the notifications. I really wasn't paying him any attention.

"Listen, you remember that nigga, Rodney? He wants to go out on a date with you."

My eyes burned with disgust. "Eww, that old ass nigga betta sit down somewhere. I ain't going nowhere with his crazy ass. But tell him he can let me borrow his Mercedes, though."

I was joking but dead ass at the same time. Rodney had a lil change on him. Word on the street is that he owns a big ass house and lives by himself. I've never seen it— and I only know him because he comes over all the time to buy weed from Nate. Rodney has a nephew named Frank who introduced them. I never met Frank, but I wish I could tell him that he made a big ass mistake by trusting my brother.

Nate was still babbling. "Trina, I'm telling ya', you go out on one date with this nigga and he's gonna be all over you. Shit, he'll probably give you the Benz. Plus a lot more."

"Why, Nate? If he gives me all this then what's in it for you?"

He sat down on the bed next to me. Anytime he does that, it means that he gotta go into a whole lecture about why I needed to do something for him. And most of the time, it's some crazy ass shit. Last time, he sent me all the way to Fat Burger just to get me to try to talk to some dude because he liked the dude's girlfriend. He wanted the girl to catch her dude in the act. Crazy part about it is, it worked.

"Listen sis," he said to me. "We're broke as fuck. Before mama died, she told me to make sure that I take care of yo' ass. This lil' check they giving me ain't cutting it. You just turned 18 last week so you got two options, either get a job or get the fuck out."

He said it with a smile, so I knew he was just teasing. "Nate, what exactly do you want me to do?" I sighed.

"A'ight, listen. I know a lotta niggas around here with money. All you gotta do is flirt with them and shit; maybe go on a couple of dates with them and once you get back to they're place, hit me up and I'll do the rest."

"Do the rest like what?"

"You know... Rob they muthafuckin' ass. You don't go out to the clubs or nothing so they won't recognize you as my little sister. I'll show you where they hang and what to say. Follow my lead and we gonna be stacking cheese in no time."

"Is that what you're trying to do with Rodney?"

"Hell yeah," he cheesed. "His ass will be easy. You can rob him your damn self. He gave my homegirl,

Ta'Shonda his safe code. She was fucking with him for a minute. She actually gave the nigga the pussy, but yeen gotta do all that. All you gotta do is go up to that pool hall down the street and he gon' come holla at you. Usually, it's nothing but old folks in there so when he sees someone young like you, his ass is gonna try to jump all over you. Just go back to his crib and when he's not paying attention, go to the safe and wipe that shit clean. She said he keeps all his money in there."

It sounded too good to be true, but we were truly broke so I was willing to take my chances. "Fuck it. I'm game."

Entry 1

My First Kill

I slowly lifted my dress and danced for him before taking it off completely. His dick rose when he saw my thongs. This nigga was ready. Once I took my panties off, I tossed them at him. He was enjoying himself, but I had to fake every moment. I'm just not the one to let any and everybody see my shit. I had a purpose though, and all that mattered was me fulfilling it by getting him hooked just by looking at it. He damn sure wasn't getting any.

I had him right where I wanted him. I climbed on the bed and spread my legs open and rubbed my pussy. His eyes stayed focus. "Girl, we gonna have to take this to the Jacuzzi," he declared, while rubbing his hands together. "Now bring that ass in there with me."

I gave a forced smile. Pfft, this nigga probably wouldn't last two seconds. Anyway…he left out and went to the bathroom. Once I heard the water running, I was ready to make my move. I put my dress on and began searching the room for his safe. I couldn't find it, so I texted Nate to see where Ta'Shonda saw it at, but he didn't text back quick enough. Finally, I found it in his closet. Just as I went to my purse to get the combination, I heard the water cut off, then heard water splashing as he got in. I opened the safe and my eyes lit up when I saw the cash. Instead of taking it and leaving, I stood there like a dumb ass and counted it. Twenty stacks. *Damn, it's about to be a wonderful day.* I said to myself.

His ass was so dumb. He barely knew me and had his wallet, keys, and phone all on the dresser. I wasn't into credit cards just yet, so I left the wallet. But since the phone was an iPhone, I snatched that up too.

"You coming, bae?" he shouted from the bathroom.

My chest burned in panic for a second. I had to think of something quick to say. "Yeah, give me a sec; let me take my clothes off."

SHIT. He had already seen me take my clothes off. I didn't know if he comprehended that, but I didn't want to take any chances. I made sure that the money was secure in my purse and I bolted for the door.

When I got to the living room, I heard splashing again then quick footsteps going back into the room. Fuck! I left the safe open too. I maybe had a few seconds to get out.

I started pulling on the doorknob, only to realize that it had a double-sided deadbolt on it. This muthafucka done locked me in. The keys were in his room, still sitting on the dresser. *Pull yourself together, and get the fuck out, Katrina.*

The kitchen was to my left and there was a sliding door over there also. That was probably my only way out. I ran over to it and pulled the handle, but it was stuck. I sat my purse down and pulled that bitch with all my might. Finally, it opened.

"Katrina, where you at, bitch!" he shouted. His tone alone had me spooked. I ignored him and as soon as I picked my purse up to go out the door, I heard a gun-cocking sound.

"Bitch, get yo' ass back in here with my shit." He said it as calm as hell. Almost as if he was used to talking to women like that. He snatched me away from the door and slung my little ass to the ground. Next thing you know, I was met with punches and kicks. I could feel my face swelling up after every blow.

My brother gave me a knife just in case I needed it, but it was in my purse which got thrown several feet away.

"See bitch, I liked you," he said, while still beating my ass. "I wasn't gonna do you like I did Deja and

Diamond—but now, I'ma make sure you feel the same pain that they did. I'ma fuck you real good and when I get tired of you, I'ma bury yo' ass right next to them."

Man, I was in some deep shit. Deja and Diamond were the two eighteen-year-old girls that went missing about a year ago. They used to wait tables at a restaurant not too far from where he stayed. Dammit. My brother sent me to rob the wrong person. I needed to make a move quick if I wanted to get out of there.

After he was satisfied with the bruising, he climbed on top of me and tried to force his dick in. I tried to force him off me, but he grabbed my arms and overpowered me with ease. My only hope was to outsmart him. He seemed to be into that gory type of shit.

"Wait let me get comfortable," I said to him. I smiled at him and it gave off a sign of submission. I don't know if he was just horny as fuck or crazy as fuck, but my smiled calmed him down. I slid off my dress while he laid on his back. I got on top of him and his dick penetrated my pussy. He closed his eyes, enjoying my goodies.

My purse was in reach now, so all I had to do was lean forward. While he was sucking my titties, I unzipped it and pulled out my knife. I stopped abruptly then held it up to his throat.

He opened his eyes. "Wait," he cried. "I wasn't going to hurt—"

I sliced his ass. Blood rushed out of his mouth and throat. I was scared as shit at first, but oddly, the more he gagged, I started enjoying the shit. Images of Deja and Diamond popped up in my head. He did them wrong and his ass was paying the price. I raised the knife as high as I could and brought it back down again. Not a breath was left in him.

Entry 2

The Beginning of a Come-Up

It took me nearly two weeks to come back home after killing his ass. I stayed at a hotel in Long Beach. I was scared that the cops would know I did it. I knew Nate was probably worried like hell, but I didn't want to take that chance. I didn't even call him to tell him I was okay.

When I finally did go home, he was sitting at the table counting money. When he saw me, he sat the money down and raised his head up at me. "Girl, where the hell you been?" he shouted. "I was worried like a muthafucka. I heard Rodney got popped the same night I sent you over there. Have you been watching the news? They found bodies in that nigga backyard. I was praying you weren't one of them."

Nate ain't prayed a day in his damn life. "I killed him," I said, walking all the way up to him. "But you don't seem too worried, you over here counting money instead of looking for me."

I loved my brother to death, but it was true. His main love was the green. I'm sure he was worried about me but he probably cared more about me getting the money. I had my phone shut off the whole time that I was gone.

I took off my shades and showed him the healing bruises.

"Damn, sis, he did that shit to you and you were able to get free *and* kill him? I'm raising you right then."

He was dead ass serious. Nate didn't have a heart. If someone wronged him, I doubt they would live another day to talk about it.

"Let's just say I distracted him," I replied. "I made my move and stabbed the shit out of him. He had to pay for beating my ass and killing those two girls."

Nate turned his face up. "What girls? You talking about the bodies they found?"

"Yep, Deja and Diamond. You remember when they went missing, right?"

"Yeah, I remember. Muthafuckas used to say that he was the one who did it. Damn."

"Yep, he said it out of his own mouth."

"So, where the money?"

See, I knew it. It wasn't long before he asked about the money. "It's all in my bag, Nate. I only had to pay the owner of the hotel $100 dollars for the whole two weeks. I made up a story about me getting abused by my boyfriend and he fell for it."

"Keep the rest." He said it like he really meant it. I had to raise an eyebrow. "Really?" I asked as I tilted my head so he could see my eyes through the sunglasses.

"Yes, really. We're 'bout to be in business now, sis. I want you to take some of that money and get some more clothes. Some of that expensive shit. It's a lot of niggas out there who ballin' like Rodney was. For the easy ones, you can handle them just like you did him. Yeen gotta go around dropping bodies left and right, though. Just try to outsmart them and rob their ass blind. And for the real gangstas, you're gonna need my help. When you get to their crib, just text me. I'll come through and take everything."

"Not every nigga carries cash on them, Nate." I really liked his ideas but just wanted to make sure he thought it all through.

"Listen, sis. If you at a nigga's house, it's gonna be something valuable in there. I mean, you could look over their shoulders and get pin numbers, credit card info, passwords and a bunch of shit. Let them wine and dine you and gain your trust. Even if it takes a hot minute, we got all the time in the world. Get you a few at a time. And I'ma get you a strap just in case some shit goes down again. That knife shit ain't gonna work with everybody."

"Bet," I replied while nodding.

I looked around my room and saw how we were living. We needed a come up. Plus, I hope that I run into some no-good guys like Rodney. I plan on taking everything they own; including their lives if I have to. Who wants to be my next victim?

Entry 3

Ice

Club Obsession was always poppin' on Fridays. This was the only time I would venture off to Hollywood. I had my hair done, my nails done; I was as fly as I could be.

They didn't check for I.D. either. With my lipstick and make-up on, I could easily go for twenty-five.

I got there early so I could get a table by the door. They were first come, first served. I wanted every nigga to see me when they walked in.

I sipped on some wine while I waited for the club to fill up. Around eleven, all the broke muthafuckas were already inside because it was free before then. The big ballers usually didn't make an appearance until well after midnight.

After all the *damn you fine, hey lil' mama* ass niggas left me alone, that's when the real spenders came in. Nate told me to look for a dude named Ice. I've never heard of him, but apparently, he was well known. He told me that the DJ would announce his arrival. He also said that he would walk in alone but be greeted by a large crowd of people.

A little after midnight, I saw him. At least I was almost certain it was. He was tall, chocolate and had that Cali swag. Crisp outfit, iced out, nice shoes and a well-trimmed beard.

Honestly, I was kinda hoping it wasn't him. Shit, I didn't want to rob a nigga as fine as him. I was thinking about getting him in the bed with me.

"Ice in the building!" The DJ announced. He raised his hand to acknowledge himself. Within seconds, the crowd flocked to him. I kept my eyes on him, but was thrown off when someone came up to my table. I saw them out the corner of my eye and I was about to trip, but then I heard my name. "Trina!" a voice said.

I looked and it was a female. Not just any female, it was my damn best friend, Toya! We go way back. I've fucked with this bitch since we were like eight years old.

"What are you doing here?" I asked her.

"Oh, I came here with Kareem and the rest of the crew. His birthday is tonight. They already left, though. I was about to leave too until I saw you over here."

"Well, sit down, bitch," I said to her jokingly. I could tell that she was tired but I wanted to catch up with her. It had been a minute since we hung out.

We talked for a good while, but I had to focus back on Ice. I saw too many ugly ass hoes around him. I had to do something to get his attention. He was leaning against the bar, so I got up and walked over there. When I was directly in front of him, I brushed up against him slowly. I then leaned forward on the bar and watched as he stared at my ass. It seemed as if none of those other hoes mattered to him anymore.

When the bartender came over to me, I asked him for a food menu. I took it and started walking back to the table. Ice gently grabbed my arm when I passed him again. "Hey ma," he said while his eyes were glued to my chest. "I got a table over there if you want to join me. I can order you some food too."

I gently pulled away. "Sorry, I got my own table," I replied.

I knew I had him. All I had to do was play that "hard to get" game. I walked back to my table with a big ass smile on my face.

"Girl, Ice is about to come over here!" Toya screamed.

I turned around and saw him then looked back at her. "Damn, you know him, too?" I whispered.

"Girl, who doesn't know him? He be out here rapping and shit. He used to be cool with Kareem and Terrell. Slim knows him too."

I shook my head. I hated when people call Nate, Slim. I love my brother but there ain't nothing *Slim* about his ass. Anyways, Ice walked over to our table and sat beside me like he knew me or something. My plan was working really good but I gave him a look like, 'nigga please.'

He asked was I there with a man and I told him I was single. Then he took the menu away from me and pulled out a stack of cash and told us we can order whatever we wanted. Toya's crazy ass ordered a burger, some wings and a side salad. I tried to act boujee and ordered some shit I couldn't pronounce. The waitress said that it had chicken in it so that was good enough for me.

Ice got up a few times, but for the most part, he stayed there talking to us. He had a pretty good, *talk-game* but I could tell that he was full of shit.

*****

The place shut down at 2 a.m. By then, this nigga was kissing my neck and rubbing my thighs. Jealous hoes walked past, and I got a kick out of it.

"What you gettin' into after the club?" He asked as we got up.

"My bed," I responded. He was back to staring at my chest again so I covered my top with my sweater. I don't mind a nigga staring at me, but if you're holding a conversation with me, at least have the respect to look me in my eyes.

I ended up giving him my number. I told him to hit me up whenever. I had a feeling that he was going to call me that same night.

Right after he left, Toya and I got up to leave. She had no idea what I was involved in. That was my girl but I didn't want her knowing that side of me. If I got caught up in some shit, I didn't want it to affect her.

About an hour later, after I was in my bed, Ice sent me a text asking if we could meet up. I was tired but didn't want to pass up on the opportunity. He sent me the address and I told him I was on my way. Once I got in the car, I sent Nate the address.

When I was about half way there, Nate called me. I knew it had to be a change of plans or something. "Yeah, Nate," I answered, clearly annoyed.

"Hey, Trina, I'on think I can make it anytime soon. I'm way across town. Just see how the nigga living. Make him feel comfortable and we'll rob his ass another time."

"Uh-uh, Nate. Listen, I got out my damn bed for this. What the fuck am I going do over his house tonight if I'm not there to rob him? He for damn sho' not getting any pussy. My period is on."

"Girl, I'ain' tryin' to hear all that shit," he chuckled. "I'll tell you what… Let me hit this other lick real quick and I'll be there in about an hour. In the meantime, just sweet talk the nigga or some shit. Rub his back or whatever. Just don't leave till I get there."

"Whatever, Nate."

When I arrived at the address, I almost turned around. I was in the parking lot of some cheap ass hotel. I looked through my texts to double check the address. It was right. This nigga really was trying me like I'm some kind of hoe.

Since I was already there and Nate was on the way, I decided to go with it as planned. I knocked on the door and he answered in his boxers. His dick was halfway out.

He hugged me and let me in. I sat on the armchair. To my right, I saw two duffels bags that were open. One had money and the other had weed.

"This where I stay at from time to time," he smiled, once he saw me staring at the bags. "A nigga like me gotta stay low-key; feel me?"

Yeah, I feel ya alright. That money and weed was about to be mine. I texted Nate and told him what I saw. He replied and said he was on the way ASAP.

Ice laid down on the bed. He pulled his dick out and started stroking it. "So, we gon' fuck or what? You over there sitting down all shy and shit."

I twisted my face at him. "Fuck? That's how you talk to females?"

He grinned. "Shidd, usually I-ain' gotta say nothing to y'all hoes. Bitches throw they self at me. My name Ice, sweetheart. Consider yourself lucky to even be over here. Gone head and show ya boy what you working with."

Lucky? In this dirty ass hotel? I wanted to curse his ass out, but I didn't want to get kicked out before Nate got there. "I can't. I'm on my period."

"And? Da fuck that mean?"

"It means I ain't fucking. You's a nasty ass nigga if you want some bloody pussy."

"Bitch, what the fuck you say to me?"

Now, he was about to get it. I had been called one too many bitches.

"Look, did I tell you I was about to fuck you, nigga? No. And yo momma the bitch. Let me get the fuck outta here."

I shook my head in disgust and headed for the door. He jumped up off the bed so damn quick and before I could react, he picked me up and threw me on the bed. "Bitch you fenna give me some pussy," he declared, ripping my clothes. "Y'all hoes want a nigga to buy y'all dinner and shit but when it comes to giving up the pussy, y'all be acting funny. Not today, though."

I tried my best to fight him off, but he was too strong. When he got to my panties, he saw the pad. He smacked his teeth and put his dick in my face. "You bout to give me *something*," he said, trying to force it in my mouth.

I laid all the way back and stroked it. Once the nigga relaxed and started moaning, I punched him in his nuts. He squinted in pain and rolled off the bed like a lil bitch. I took my chances and tried to run for the door again

"Bring yo' ass here bitch," he ordered. I heard the gun click, so I knew what time it was. I turned around and he was on his knees, holding the gun up.

Not again…"Look, just let me go," I pleaded. Wasn't sure how much it would help but I tried anyway.

"Nah, bitch. It's something strange about you," he said while standing to his feet. "I saw you looking at me from the time I walked in that club. You must be plotting something. I'ma figure it out, and in the meantime, you about to suck this dick. You got five seconds to bring that ass over here."

As soon as he said "one," the door burst open. Nate had the gun in his hand and lit his ass up.

"You ok, sis?" he asked, running to my side. I was balled up in the corner. The gunshots were loud as fuck.

"I'm fine."

Once I got to my feet, we took everything of value that he had in his room. He had more money and weed in his trunk and we took all of it. After that, we drove back home.

Nate counted everything and sat next to me when he was done. He seemed angry. "Why you looking at me like that?" I asked.

"You gotta make sure you have your strap at all times, Trina. I told you it's niggas out here that would kill yo' ass without question. Make sure you keep that shit by your side."

I nodded. He was right. It was time for me to stop fucking around like a rookie. I have to show them niggas who's in charge.

Entry 4

Tavious

Within a day or two, they closed down that raggedy ass hotel. Apparently, there had been several other crimes and murders and the city had enough.

That same day, a crowd drew in near the hotel to mourn the loss of Ice… And yes, I was there. I'm not quite sure why I came, though. In my eyes, I couldn't see why the people loved him so much. I'm sure I wasn't the first girl he's done that too.

While there, I tried to keep my distance. I'm pretty sure some of the same people there mourning him, were in the club last Friday.

After backing up as far as I could, I turned to my right, and saw someone looking at me. All it took was a brief moment of locking eyes with him before he came over to me.

"So, you know Ice, huh?" he asked.

"I've seen him before," I responded just before the adrenaline came rushing in.

"Yeah… ok. I thought I recognized you. He was sitting at your table at Club Obsession the night he was killed."

I didn't get the sense of accusation in his voice. I felt that he was just mourning a friend. I went along with it. "Yeah, we had a nice, long conversation that night. I guess he liked me or something."

"I can see why," he said while rubbing his hands together.

"Do they know who did it?" I asked to make sure he didn't think it was me.

"Nah, unfortunately this hotel ain't have no cameras or nothing. Ice was my dude, but he was so damn careless. They found him half-naked, so it was probably one of those bitches he knew. Excuse my language."

"It's all good," I replied. "He did seem like a really cool dude. It's so unfortunate."

I relaxed. The conversation became much more interesting. He told me that his name was Tavious and I told him mine. We clicked. He asked if I wanted to get something to eat. We went to a diner not too far from the hotel.

As we sat and ate, I was trying to get a feel for him. He seemed different than Ice, but knowing that they were boys, I knew he had to be similar some type of way. Tavious was taller, sexier and seemed to know how to talk to a female much better than Ice did. I didn't mind giving him the booty if it led to it.

"You wanna go to my crib?" he asked. "It ain't what you thinking, though. I just live right up the street. We can chill for a bit but if you wanna go out somewhere else, then we can do that, too."

"We can go to your place," I shrugged.

I followed him. He had a motorcycle and a SUV parked in the garage. He was already in a BMW so I could tell he had a lil' change. I just knew he had a wife or something. Ain't nam' nigga that fine with that much paper gonna be walking around single.

"You want something to drink?" he asked once we sat down.

"Do you have wine?"

"Yeah, I might." He got up and came back with a shot of Crown for him and a glass of Moscato for me. He sat on the other sofa and cut the TV on. His phone rang about ten minutes later and this nigga had the audacity to walk to the back to take the call. I know I heard a female voice on the other end so when he came back, I made sure I questioned him.

"Umm, tell yo' lil' hoes that Katrina over here. They can have you later." The corner of my mouth turned up as I awaited his response. Really, I was just teasing him since I barely knew him, but it did feel good to see his reaction. He put his hand on his chin and smiled, showing his gold teeth.

"Man, I-ain' got no hoes. That was my sister. Talking bout she needs me to pay her rent this month. I done paid it like three months straight already."

I wasn't sure if he saw it or not, but my eyes damn sholl' widened. This nigga got money to pay his mortgage and somebody else's rent? I felt like I hit the jackpot. And I wasn't on any robbing shit either. I could see myself as his girl.

"So, where does your sister live?" I asked. I tried to make myself sound interested, but really, I was just trying to see what type of money he was dishing out.

"Oh, shid she stays all the way in damn Philadelphia. She works for my uncle, Lawrence."

"Well, obviously your uncle Lawrence not paying her enough."

"Yeah, he's a cheap ass dude. Matter of fact, he lives here. She's running one of his clubs up there. I keep telling her to bring her ass back home but she doesn't want to live with me no more. She said I be in her business too much."

"And you probably do," I replied. "My brother is the same way. We live together now and he always in my business. I don't blame your sister. Philly is a good place to be. I wouldn't mind moving there one day."

He laughed at me. Everyone laughs at me when I mention moving to Philly. They ask me why would I trade the sun and beach for snow and congestion. It's not so much the city itself that I like, I just want to be somewhere different. I had never been there before but it's just a city that stood out to me anytime I see it on T.V.

Tavious was sitting on the other sofa acting shy. Maybe he was thinking about other things, but I wanted to shift the mood. I cut the lights off and sat next to him. He put his arm around me, and I put my hand through his tank top and started rubbing his chest. He reached over and started kissing me. He had some big, sexy ass lips and his kiss game was on point.

He took his beater off and tried to unfasten my pants, but I had to stop him right there. My period was still on. I wasn't going to leave him hanging, especially since I was the one who came on to him. I unzipped his pants and pulled it out. I then massaged it and worked my mouth down to it.

He likes me, he got money; I'm gonna have fun with this nigga.

Entry 5

Jamarcus

Me and Tavious had been kicking it for a few months now, and I kept it a secret from my brother, but he somehow found out about it. Apparently, he knew him. He stormed in the house one day and questioned me about it. "Trina, you fucking with that nigga, Tay?"

Tay was what they called him in the streets. I can tell by my brother's tone that he wasn't happy about it.

"Yeah, why?"

"Girl, I had to hear from the streets that you his ol' lady now. This nigga sitting on a buncha green and yeen' clean that nigga out yet? Da fuck is you waiting on?"

I shook my head. Nate never cared about feelings. It was always about the paper. I was happy with Tay and I didn't want to let him take that away from me.

"It ain't always about the money, NATE. I really like this dude."

"Trina, listen; you supposed to be on a mission. Fuck feelings. We need to get this money. I'm tired of slangin' and shit."

"Look, I want the money too, Nate. I'm just saying, not with Tay. When I met him, I wasn't on that type of shit anyway. We met at the lil' memorial they had for Ice."

"Whatever," he said while giving a dismissive wave. "When you gonna get back to this 'getting paper' mentality?"

"Soon," I replied. "Real soon."

Nate was right. I had been slipping a lil' and the money needed to be made. I told him that I would go out that night. Tavious and I had plans, but I called him up to cancel.

*****

There was a lounge near the airport that I had in mind. It was low-key and not much was going on out there since it was a Tuesday. I figured that it would be the perfect spot to find some random dude who had money. I played it smart this time and took an Uber. I grew tired of riding in separate cars and shit. It's best that I ride home with whoever I met and then get my brother to come get me.

When I got there, I saw a few nice cars parked in valet. I walked in with a huge smile on my face. An instant rush of excitement hit me when I walked through the door. There were several men inside sitting by themselves. Before I decided where to sit, I scanned the room to try to get a feel of some of them. I wasn't about to just go sit by some random nigga. I had a good eye at spotting wedding rings from a distance. Married men were the ones who spent the most money.

As I stood there, I felt someone step into my space. "Hey, beautiful, how you doing?" he greeted as I turned around. He was a heavy-set dude but was well dressed in slacks and smelled good too. I decided to entertain it for a minute.

"I'm good," I smiled.

"Well, I just wanted to introduce myself. I saw you standing up here for a minute and didn't know if you were looking for someone."

I did another quick scan of the room and this dude was the best dressed. I remember seeing an old school Impala outside and he seemed like the type who drove one.

"No, I-ain' looking for nobody," I replied. "Just trying to see where to sit."

"I got a table over here if you wanna join me. I can get you a drink and we can just talk or whatever."

The way he grinned and licked his lips, I knew that *talking* wasn't on his mind. It was more of doing the *whatever* part he mentioned.

He told me that his name was Jamarcus. Once we sat, he tried to be slick and slide his ring off his finger and put it in his pocket. I didn't call him out on it because I really didn't give a damn who he was going home to.

Our conversation was good and what made it even better was how he bragged on all the shit he had. That's the problem with most niggas; they tell you all this shit to try to impress you. What he didn't realize was, I was plotting. He started talking about his Impala so I was able to confirm that it was his car that I saw outside.

He kept pulling out his knot every time we ordered a drink. I sent my brother a text and told him that I had one. I was able to sneak a pic of him and send it to him too. Nate texted back and said that he didn't want me to handle it myself. I wasn't sure if it was because dude was bigger than me but I told him cool.

"What you doing after you leave here?" he asked.

There goes that saying again. They may say it different but it all means the same. "Nothing. I'ma have to catch a cab back to my house and gotta get up for work in the morning."

"Yeen gotta do that, sweetheart. I can give you a ride home. We can chill for a lil bit and then I'll drop you off."

"Cool," I said while smiling. I definitely wanted him to feel like I was interested in him. I honestly think I sounded a lil' too excited.

Before leaving the bar, he downed two shots of liquor. He had already been drinking all night. Valet brought him his car and we got in. The ride was even nicer up close. He had candied paint, 24's and a few TVs inside. Once we pulled out of the parking lot, he drove around for a lil bit. He didn't seem like he had any particular place to go.

"You smoke?" he asked.

"Occasionally."

"Well, I was about to light up if you don't mind."

"Nope, not at all." We stopped at an abandoned parking lot. He lit up the weed and we took turns. The weed had him more relaxed and flirty. He started saying all type of shit to me about how he would do this and that. I knew it was probably just talk.

I sent Nate a text. I wasn't sure what street we were on, but I knew that we were not too far away from the bar.

I looked around and saw a few landmarks. When I sent it to Nate, he was able to figure out where we were. He said he was only 10 minutes away.

"Who you texting?" he asked. You gotta get back to your man or something? I see you texting and then looking around at the surroundings. That nigga ain't about to come after me is he?"

I smirked. "Child, please. I need to be worrying about your wife. Don't think I didn't see that ring earlier. I don't need no drama."

He smiled it off. I knew deep down, he was paranoid. I had to give him a reason to relax. I took off my seatbelt and started rubbing on his thigh. I then unzipped his pants and pulled out his dick. He was calm and puffing the blunt. I started licking it slowly to keep him relaxed. I was hoping Nate would hurry up and come through so I could be on my way.

"Shid, I want to see what that pussy working with," he insisted, while grabbing my head.

Fuck it. I slid my panties off and climbed on top of him. For an older dude, his stroke game was on point.

As I was enjoying the sex, out of nowhere, he threw me off of him. "The fuck gonna on?" he said while giving me a dirty look. I thought I was squishing his nuts or something the way he looked at me. I knew it was serious when he pulled out the gun. "Oh, so you one of them shady bitches, huh?"

"What? What did I do?"

I looked out the window and saw Nate's car. He should've pulled up more covertly. We were the only ones in the parking lot.

"I see that nigga sneaking up," Jamarcus said as he looked out the back window. "I'm about to fuck this nigga up then come back and deal with yo' shady ass."

He pushed me and I fell back down. He jumped out the car to confront Nate. Nate didn't see him initially, so I screamed to get his attention. Seconds later, bullets started flying. I couldn't tell if Nate was hit or not, but he ran for cover. Jamarcus retreated back to the car. I pulled out my gun just before he opened the car door. I kept it on my side.

As soon as he got in, he put his gun away and threw the gear in drive. He sped out of the parking lot. "Who the fuck was that nigga?" he said while mean-mugging me. "You were really trying to set me up?"

"No, I don't even know who you're talking about." I pleaded. "I just started screaming when I saw him. Could've been a jack-boy. Did you shoot him?"

"Nah, his punk ass ran away before I could hit him."

My mama always told me that I was good at acting before she died. I was fake crying and it convinced him.

"Let's get you home," he said to me. "I'ma come back later with my niggas. We gonna catch his ass. I saw what kinda car he drive and I swear I've seen him before."

Jamarcus may have had gang ties, so I didn't want to run the risk of Nate getting caught up in anything. I had to end it right then and there. They would find Nate in no time. He's easy to describe, with his big ass.

When we approached a traffic light, I looked through the side mirror and noticed that Nate was behind us, traveling at a safe distance. The light turned red and as soon as we stopped, Nate switched lanes and was now on Jamarcus's side. He was so into getting me home, that he didn't notice him. I nodded at Nate to let him know that I was in control. Jamarcus happened to see my movement. When he turned to me, he saw me looking to his left. He turned his head and spotted Nate. He tried to grab his gun, but I quickly raised mine before he could. I pulled the trigger and the power of the gun was so strong, it made my hands raise up. The gun dropped on the floor and when I looked over at Jamarcus, he had a hole next to his ear. He made a sound then bled out.

I was in shock for a second. Nate ran over and started searching the car. "Go get in my car," he said to me. "Drive off and meet me at the crib."

"How are you gonna get back?" I asked.

He looked at me and grinned. "Girl, this is a six-fo. I'm gonna toss his big ass out and keep it for myself. Danny at the chop shop can paint it and clean it up for me."

Luckily, there were no other cars nearby at the time. It was late, anyway. I helped Nate pull him out. Jamarcus had some extra clothes in the trunk so Nate used them to cover up some of the blood on the seat. I then got in Nate's car and drove away.

*****

Nate took a while to get home. As soon as he walked in, he slammed the door and sat on the sofa.

"What's wrong, Nate?"

He shook his head and exhaled. "Man, that dude that you just killed was one of Frank's homeboys. He was beefing with Kareem and Terrell and I guarantee that Frank gonna think that they had something to do with this shit."

"Who the fuck is Frank?" I asked. "And whoever he is, I'm sure Kareem can handle them."

Nate let off another deep sigh. "That ain't the point, Trina. Frank is the nephew of Rodney; the man you killed a while back. I barely know him but we got a few mutual connects. One being this nigga named Chris. I can't let this shit fuck up my money so I'ma have to get the word out that Kareem did this shit."

"So, you gonna lie on Kareem?"

"Yeah, but Kareem won't be worried. I'on think Frank dumb enough to step to him anyway. And you need to take off that damn necklace because if Frank sees that shit, he gonna know you had something to do with his uncle's murder."

I did get that necklace from Rodney. I didn't know how Nate knew, but since he did, I felt that it was best to take it off; for now. Rodney gave it to me that night we hung out. He said that it was his mother's. I think he really liked me. It was crazy because I barely knew him. But, I'm gonna take the necklace off for now, and still keep it since I like it. After this shit boils down, I'll be wearing it again.

Entry 6

Chris

J woke up to a loud knock at the door. I yelled for Nate since his room was closest to the door. He didn't respond. The knock was persistent and aggressive so I had no choice but to get out of bed and see who it was. I walked past Nate's room and he wasn't there. Before I got to the door, I looked out the window and his car was gone. I did see a dark colored Chevy sitting in the drive way. Whoever was at the door was still knocking.

"Who is it?" I asked. I had an attitude because I looked at the clock on the wall and it was 8:06 in the morning. On a Saturday.

"Detective Caldwell." He said it calm but quickly at the same time. It was like he expected me to know who he was.

I didn't know him, and my heart dropped. *Why the fuck is a detective at my door?* I thought to myself. Well... Based on all the shit I've done, he coulda been there to arrest my ass. I just prayed that he was there for something different. I calmed myself down and opened the door.

The detective didn't look intimidating at all. When he saw me, it seemed as if he was more interested in staring at my body more than anything else.

"Can I help you?"

"Uh yes," he rectified. He shamefully looked me in my eyes as he knew I didn't appreciate him staring at me. "I'm looking for Nate Jones. People around here call him Slim. Are you his girlfriend or wife?"

"Well, I call him Nate and he's my brother. I'on know where he's at right now. May I ask why are you looking for him?"

"I just have a couple questions for him. But since you're here, do you mind if I ask you some?"

I went ahead and let him in. He seemed cool, and one thing Nate always did was make sure that nothing was left out in the house.

He took a seat on the recliner. He looked around the room at the pictures and decorations on the wall. Suddenly, his eyes stopped wandering and now he was focused on me. "Well, I came here to ask your brother some questions about a friend of his named Kareem. I got word that Nate told someone that Kareem was responsible for the murder of Jamarcus Sanders about a week ago."

I paused for a second. Probably for too long. I hope Nate wasn't turning into a snake and lying on his homeboys to the cops.

"Kareem is a good friend of ours. I don't think my brother would go around saying that he killed someone. Wherever you're getting your information, it's wrong."

"So, would your brother cover for him?"

I gave him a dirty look. "Listen, I don't know what you're talking about. All I know is, Kareem ain't gonna be running around here killing nobody either."

He could tell that I was getting agitated, so he stood up. "Sorry to disturb you. I will just come back another time. Hopefully, I can see Nate next time."

Before he left, he looked at the duffel bag on the floor in the corner. That was one of the bags that we got out of Jamarcus's trunk. We already took everything out of it but my dumbass left it in the house by mistake.

"Take care," he said to me. "Oh, and can I get your name before I go?"

"Katrina Jones."

"Thank you, Katrina," he said while walking out.

It was a quick visit. When he left, I went into a rage and called Nate to see who he had ran his mouth too. He didn't answer so I left him a voicemail letting him know that he needed to call me immediately.

Not even ten minutes later, there was another knock on the door. "Who is it?" I yelled. I was so pissed that I opened the door before hearing a response. A tall, light-skinned dude was at the door. He had braids, a white-T and a bandana on.

"Aye, Trina, let me come in real quick," he whispered. "I gotta holla at cha' in private," he said while trying to walk in.

I extended my arm out and stopped him. "Uh-uh nigga, I'on know you. You not coming in my house and how you know my name?"

"I'm Chris. Me and yo' brother started getting money together a lil' while ago and shit. I just need to holla at you about that detective who just left here."

He looked serious and if he knew the house, my name, and my brother, I figured that it was okay to trust him. I opened the door all the way and let him in.

He sat in the same seat where the detective was just at. I stayed standing up. "So, what about this detective?" I said with my arms folded.

"Look, that nigga is kinda shady. I hope yeen' tell him too much. He's been a cop for a minute but recently moved up to detective. I knew he was coming here because he had just left my house. I tried calling Slim but heen' answer so I just followed the cop around here and waited outside. When I saw you let him in, I had to come holla at you to make sure everything good."

"Yeah, everything good. Nate is just being Nate. He now got cops coming to our door. AGAIN." My frustration was showing.

"Man, listen," Chris said to me. He stood up and was all in my face as if he really wanted me to dig what he was about to tell me. "I know Slim's yo' brother, but he be on some other shit sometimes. He does a lot of shit without thinking."

"Tell me about it," I sighed.

"But don't worry about that detective. He's not even supposed to be over here anymore. He works for Long Beach now. It's something strange about him, but I don't think he'll be showing up again to be honest."

"So, how you know about him?" I asked Chris. Yeen' no snitch or nothing right? You know a lot about this dude."

Chris snickered. "I like you, Trina. And yeah, I do know a lot about this muthafucka. I've done my fair share of crazy shit back in the day, so sometimes you gotta pay muthafuckas off to keep them quiet. He only comes around when money is involved. He's not trying to solve shit. Nigga just looking for a quick dollar."

"You telling me a lot," I said while smiling. "How you know I won't snitch?"

"Oh, I can trust a girl like you. You seem like the type of female that will hold a nigga down. Ride or die chick."

"Is that so?" I blushed.

"Hell yeah. If Slim wasn't yo' brother, I would ask to take you out sometime."

"Well, I'ma tell you like I tell everybody else. First of all, his name is Nate. I hate that damn, 'Slim' name. Second of all, I'm a grown ass woman. May only be nineteen, but I am grown nevertheless."

I was kinda feeling Chris. He had a laid-back vibe to him. Maybe once I stop fooling around in this life of crime, I'll give him a chance. For now, it's back to the money. Plus, I'm sure he's getting to that money as well. Maybe we'll bump heads again one day.

$\mathcal{E}ntry$ 7

Lawrence

After a couple years of doing dumb shit, I was growing tired of it. I wasn't growing tired of the money, I was more so growing tired of Nate's ass. I was all in for robbing niggas; especially the no-good ones. The ones who were cheating on their wives and abusing women. I couldn't care less about their lives. I did feel bad for a few of the cool ones. I started catching feelings for some of them, and as soon as I gave Nate their info, they ended up dead.

I needed a new hustle. Instead of living with my brother and feeding him all my money, I decided to get my own place. During the last two years, I would say that we robbed hundreds of niggas and got a bunch of money doing it, but Nate took more than half.

He paid off my mama's house and still continued to live in it. I got a studio apartment about ten minutes up the road. I finally met a dude who had 'big-boy' money and wasn't into the streets. Most of these niggas had a lil' cash but this dude had good credit, stocks, bonds, real estate, business properties and all. We met at a seafood restaurant in Santa Monica.

We both were there alone. Every time I looked up, we locked eyes. We smiled at each other a few times. It wasn't until after he finished his food, that I realized that he was really interested in me. The waitress came over and told me that he had paid for my meal. I wanted to thank him, but when I looked up again, he was gone.

When I got outside, the cold wind slammed across my face. I wasn't ready to get in my 98' Corolla. The heat didn't work and the back window didn't roll up all the way. As I fumbled around my purse for my keys, a car pulled up beside me. It was a Bentley GT. I couldn't see who was inside of it because the tint was dark. The driver didn't get out and I just continued doing what I was doing. When I found my keys, I opened the door and was about to get in, but the person in the Bentley rolled down their window and honked at me.

I rolled my eyes. I-ain' give a damn how much money he had, the car he drove or anything else; I wasn't about to let anybody think that they could honk at me to get my attention.

When I got in the car, he honked again. He rolled his window all the way down. I still didn't recognize him. I stuck my head out the window. "Umm, can I help you?" I asked. I'm sure he heard the 'Bitch with an Attitude' in my voice.

He pointed his finger upwards. "Your phone is on top of your car."

"Oh… Thanks!" I let out quickly, with a smile. I felt pretty dumb. I grabbed it and tried to avoid eye contact.

"You look even lovelier up close," he flirted.

I bent down to see inside his car. It was the same guy who paid for my meal. He got out and walked towards me. My eyes lit up. He was quite handsome. He was older, but had a neatly trimmed, grey beard, he was about six foot three or four, and had a muscular build. Oh, and not to mention, he was dark chocolate.

"Now tell me why a beautiful lady like yourself is all alone tonight?"

I watched his lips as he spoke. I leaned on my car to try to break the nervous feeling that I had. "I'm single that's why. I don't have any friends so I decided to come here by myself."

I looked down at his hand and didn't see a ring. Not even a ring mark. I had a good eye to spot things like that.

"So, what brings you out here by yourself?" I asked.

He responded quickly. "I'm just like you. Single and no friends."

"Well, you're driving a Bentley. I know you at least got people around you. That's some big money right there."

He laughed. "Well, I own a few night clubs here and in Philadelphia. I do have a lot of associates but don't allow too many people to get close to me."

That same night, he took me to one of his clubs. It wasn't too far from where we were. It was right on the ocean and was packed. We had a few drinks and danced. It was the best night that I had in a long time.

*****

It took about three weeks for me and Lawrence to really start kicking it. I wouldn't really call it a boyfriend/girlfriend type of thing, but it was close to it. I would go to his place all the time and spent a lot of time at the clubs with him.

Unfortunately, my life wasn't changing fast enough and the 'hood' was still in me. I started taking advantage of him. I put Nate on game, and we started coming up with plots to steal from him.

One day, Lawrence asked if I wanted to go on a trip with him to Philadelphia. I had never been outside of California, so I was excited. Plus, Philly was the one place the main place on my bucket list. He booked us first-class on Delta. I had never felt so comfortable in my life. I was getting royal treatment.

We were there for a whole week, so most of the time, he was out in meetings and I was at the hotel room just chilling. He left me several credit cards and told me to buy whatever I wanted. Maaan, I bought a bunch of shit. I even bought stuff online and had it shipped to my house. I probably spent at least three grand on his cards that week. I was sure he wouldn't notice it because he was buying a bunch of stuff himself. Every day he came into the room with a new pair of shoes, clothes or something.

The night that we got back, he asked me to move in with him. I liked him but wasn't sure if I liked him *that* much.

"I love you, Katrina," he said to me. I don't think I ever heard those words from someone who meant it besides my mother.

"Do you really?" I replied. That was the best I could give him at that moment. I at least said it with a smile.

"Trina, ever since you came into my life, I've been happier than ever. I don't won't no one else besides you."

That sounded like some proposal shit. It sounded good but he didn't know anything about me. I was dark inside. I wasn't sure if love existed in me anymore. I wanted to ask him, "can you just keep fucking me good and buying me shit?" I knew that wouldn't fly with him, though. He needed confirmation that I cared for him. I had to give it to him.

"Well, Lawrence, you've changed my life as well. More than you could ever imagine."

He nodded slowly while looking into my eyes. "So, I see that you are not quite ready to tell me you love me, but how bout you still move in with me? I just want to be able to wake up to you every morning."

If he only knew. "Well, let me think about it, Lawrence. For now, I will keep my own apartment but will stay over here most nights."

"Fair enough for me, sweetheart."

I hated being this cold-hearted but the more he trusted me, the more I knew I could take from him.

*****

Within a few months, I had all of Lawrence's passwords and credit card information. He would often leave his computers unlocked and send me to the store with his wallet. I bought T.V.'s, phones, tablets and other stuff in the course of those few months. I strategized to get what I wanted. I started off with the smaller purchases. Once I noticed that he didn't say anything, I amped it up a little. I ended up getting Nate involved and he helped me sell the stuff in the streets.

Lawrence is a good man and maybe one day I will realize it and change my ways, but that may not be anytime soon. I do plan on keeping him around for a while.

Goodnight.

Entry 8

Out with the Old, In with the New

Lawrence gave me his card to go shopping for my 21st birthday which was only two weeks away. Not that it mattered, but he told me to buy whatever I wanted. I went to Century Square and found a nice dress and a few other outfits. He said that he had a few surprises for me on my birthday so I had to be prepared.

When I got ready to leave the mall, I walked past a shoe store and heard someone call my name. I looked around and saw some dude staring at me. He waved for me to come over. "Do I know you?" I asked as I got closer. "How do you know my name?"

"You're Slim's lil sister, Katrina, right?"

Now that I got a better look at him, he did look familiar, but I still didn't know who he was. "Yeah, I am, and who are you?"

"Chris. I came by the crib a couple years ago. You don't remember me?"

It then dawned on me. He was the cute light skinned dude that warned me about the police officer. Damn, that was a long time ago. "Oh, hey! How you doing?" I smiled. I gave him a hug. He held on to me for a second.

"Good. I see you left your brother's crib. Where you staying at now?"

"I got a place not too far from here." I didn't want to tell him that I moved in with my dude.

I forgot all about Chris. I'm surprised that I did, though. He was cute and we had a good convo. I wasn't even dressed like I normally would be, but he was still checking me out.

"So, you and my brother still making moves, huh? I don't talk to him that much."

He lowered his head and snickered. "Maaan, yo' brother on some other shit. Tell you the truth, if it wasn't for our connect, we probably wouldn't be fucking with each other no more."

"Same ol' Nate I see. I've only seen him a couple times in the last year or so. He moves a few things for me here and there. We're family but Nate is crazy."

"I feel ya," he replied.

We continued to walk and talk and stumbled upon a burger spot in the food court. We decided to grab a bite to eat. I felt really comfortable around him. It was a weird feeling since I barely knew him.

Chris was different in so many ways. He was hood, but had the mind of a professor or something. You could hear it in his voice. He used a lot of big words just to describe small things.

I honestly don't remember how it happened, but I ended up at his house that day. He lived in Watts, not too far from my old apartment. His mom had recently passed and she left him the house. His cousin, Henry, had also moved in with him from Atlanta.

Chris had the house decorated with portraits, and statues of famous black people. Not just rappers and celebrities, but people like Malcom X, Langston Hughes and Harriet Tubman. It was good to see someone who embraced our culture. Finally, someone who was proud to be black, and respected our ancestors.

"So, you're really into history, ha?" I asked. His eyes followed mine and he glanced at some of the pictures on the wall.

"Yeah, hopefully one day folks understand all the shit we invented and how we made, and still make a difference in this world. They like to see us as former slaves turned criminals, but that ain't how it is. It's so much more. I'll explain it to you one day."

"I can't wait to hear," I smiled.

My phone rang as we sat in the living room. It was Lawrence and I answered. I had never been the type of female to be scared to answer my phone around anyone. Especially since there wasn't a ring on my finger.

Lawrence was breathing heavily and I heard a lot of background noise. "Hey, what's wrong?" I asked.

"Trina," he rushed. "Listen, I can't explain it over the phone but I need you to come home ASAP."

The phone hung up. I don't know if he hung up or the call dropped. All I knew was that he sounded like something was wrong. "Chris, I'm sorry but I got to run," I said to him as I got up.

"Aww man, really?" he replied. "You just got here."

"Yeah, I know. My dude said he needed to holla at me about something."

"Dude?" His face frowned.

"Yeah, my dude," I replied while putting my hands up. We been kicking it for a minute."

I could tell that Chris was getting jealous but he tried to play it cool.

"Well, hopefully it won't be another three years before I see you again."

"It won't. I know where you stay now."

*****

Lawrence called me like three times asking how close I was. Each call, he sounded more worried than the last. Finally, I reached the house. When I walked in, he was packing clothes. At first, I thought they were mine. I walked up to him and moved his arm away from the suitcase. "Lawrence what the hell are you doing?"

He stopped and looked at me. He was breathing heavily and damn near in fill panic mode. He needed a second to catch his breath. "Trina, we need to leave for Philadelphia tonight. I can't explain it right now but we gotta go. It's not safe here no more for us."

"We? Not safe? For us?" After each question, I gave him a crazy ass look. Like, nigga what are you talking about.

"Listen, I booked us a flight that leaves in a few hours. Once we are in the clear, I will let you know everything."

He was still packing his suitcases and I stopped him again. "Whoa, whoa, Lawrence. No, you gonna tell me right now!" I yelled. "How you gonna up and leave your house like that? You aren't making any sense."

He seemed like he wanted to tell me but he kept looking around the room, avoiding eye contact. He was shaking uncontrollably. I had never seen this man so scared in my life. Once he saw that I wasn't about to start packing without an answer, he walked away and went back to his suitcase.

I sat on down on the couch. I was starting to get a little nervous, but I kept telling myself to calm down. What could he possibly be running from? An ex? The IRS? Lawrence wasn't involved in any street life as far as I knew, so that didn't cross my mind.

Once he got his suitcases packed, he sat them by the door. He then walked over to me and handed me a business card. "Listen Katrina. I have to go. I'll be in Philly and the info on this card is the only way you'll be able to reach me. Please don't share this with anyone."

"So, you're really gonna leave like that? What are you gonna do with your house? Your night clubs?"

"Baby, I'm sorry but I can't be here anymore. I got into business with some bad people and they started sending out threats. I almost lost my life over my nightclub."

My phone rang and it startle the shit out of Lawrence. He tried to calm down but it didn't work. He kissed me on the cheek and grabbed his bags. He left out without saying another word to me. I left a minute or two after him. If someone was really after him, I wasn't going to stay and find out who.

Entry 9

Back Where I Started

Without an apartment to my name anymore and Lawrence gone, I went back home with my brother. I didn't want to, but I didn't have a choice. I figured that I would only be there for a couple of months anyway.

The same day that I moved in, he had the nerve to come in my room with an attitude. "So, I heard you fucking with Chris. How long has this been going on?"

I rolled my eyes. It wasn't none of his business who I was messing with. "Yeah, so? We've been kicking it for a minute." Normally, I would beat around the bush or lie about it, but ever since Lawrence left, Chris and I had been getting pretty close and it was time for Nate to know.

"Well, just be careful. You know Chris roll with them killas."

"Boy, please. Chris ain't done nothing that you and I haven't done. I'm a grown woman and can handle myself. Thank you."

"Whatever, Trina," he pouted as he walked off. I didn't know why he didn't want me talking to Chris but that was his problem.

After leaving out, he went in the room with his girlfriend, Kandy. She moved in a few months ago. Although they got along good, they couldn't have been any more opposite. I've known Kandy for a minute. I used to cheat off her math tests in school. She was quiet, reserved and shy. She never really talked to anyone besides me and Toya. It was a few times that some of the older girls would talk shit about her and I helped her out a few times. They used to pick on her about her weight. She has lost a lot since then, but she told me that those bad names still haunt her.

Her real name in Kandice. She goes by Kandy because that was how her grandma used to pronounce it. Her grandma raised her and had a heart attack during our senior year. Kandy was supposed to go off to college but decided to stay home and go to the local community college. She dropped out when she met my brother. I hated the fact that she would allow him to slow down her goals.

Kandy didn't know a thing about the streets. She didn't drink nor smoke. Didn't like altercations and she barely even said a curse word. Since she was dumb enough to move in with my brother, it wouldn't be long before he gets her involved in some shit.

They met while I was living with Lawrence. Kandy saw him at the mall and recognized him as my big brother. She then asked about me and that's how things took off with them. Up until her moving in, I hadn't seen her since high school. Back then, she was chubby and young, so my brother wasn't checking for her.

I couldn't worry about their relationship too much since I had a new man in Chris. I love being with him because he knows how to keep his business life and personal life separate.

I did meet his closest homeboys; Frank and Mike. It was brief. Kinda like hey and bye. Chris didn't know too much about my past life. He thought that I was a good girl, so he wanted to keep me out of the streets.

Entry 10

I'm out

This was out of the norm, but I decided to surprise Chris by showing up at his house. We already had plans for later that night, but I was sitting in the house bored and wanted to see him sooner. When I pulled up to his house, he was outside arguing with some older woman. Well, she was arguing with him, and he was just standing there listening with his arms folded. I was about to jump in it and say something, but she reminded me of my mama. My mama always put it in my head to respect the elderly. I just waited by my car until she got done. Before she walked off, she looked me up and down and rolled her eyes.

"What's her problem?" I asked Chris.

He brushed it off with a downward wave. "Ahh, nothing. That's Ms. Shirley. She lives across the street. She was telling me that we be having the music too loud some times and how my cousin Henry need to stop smoking weed outside."

"She looked like she was ready to beat that ass," I joked.

"While you playing, Ms. Shirley is 'bout that life. She used to sell dope with her husband back in the day."

"Well, why you outside, anyway?" I asked him. "And you should be getting dressed. You know we're going out tonight."

"Girl, you ain't supposed to be here till eight. It's only five now, so I'll get dressed around seven. And I'm out here because my boys are supposed to come through and holla at me."

He didn't say it, but I know that he was disappointed that I came early. He probably wanted to hang out with his boys, but I didn't give a damn. It was my time. Just as we were about to go in the house, a car pulled up. It was the same two guys that he always talked to; Frank and Mike. They stayed in the car, but this time I got a good look at their faces. Apparently, they got a good look at me as well because Frank couldn't keep his eyes off of me. It wasn't a lustful look either, it was just a blank stare. I almost cursed his ass out but I decided to chill. I didn't have time for them dudes.

Once they started smoking, I went in the house. I didn't want to be around all that. "Alright, now. Ms.

Shirley gonna come back out here and kick your ass!" I shouted. "She just told you about that weed!" Chris and Mike laughed. Frank was still looking crazy.

I went inside and played on my phone. They were loud as hell. I overheard Chris talking about an incident that happened a while back. He told them that Antonio sent him to kill a dude named Blaze, but Blaze found out about it and left town for Philadelphia. He also said Antonio took all of Blaze's dope and took over his nightclub, but he still wanted him dead.

He mentioned my brother, too. They were talking about moving weight and taking over territories. Listening to all of that made me sick to my stomach. Chris was just like everyone else. I loved him but realized that I needed to get away. I knew he sold weed and dope, but I didn't know that he was out here killing people. The way he spoke about it was too calm. It was definitely something that he'd done before. I had already killed enough people throughout the years and I wasn't about to get sucked back into that life.

Since I've been with him, I had been staying out of the streets. I haven't been fucking with Nate either. I just wanted peace.

He came inside about twenty minutes later. I was in his room gathering all the things that I had over there. He didn't even know what I was doing. He just went straight to his closet. "You think I should dress up or just wear some jeans and J's."

I ignored him and continued getting my stuff together.

"You heard me, bae?"

Still silent.

He walked over and tried to put his arm around me but I pulled away.

"Damn, Trina, what's your problem?" he shouted. "I wasn't even out there with them that long."

"This ain't got shit to do with your homeboys, Chris! I'm just tired of this shit!"

Tears fell down my face, then I started boohoo crying. I could feel my soul burning. It felt like every person that I've robbed, killed or done wrong, was somehow attacking me from within.

Poor Chris didn't know what was wrong with me. He sat next to me and spoke softly. "Hey, tell me what's wrong, bae? Did I do something to hurt you?"

I took a deep breath and told him exactly how I felt. "Chris, I've done a lot of shit in my life and I just can't be around the killing and drugs anymore. I've always had dreams that I wouldn't live to see thirty. If that's true, then I don't want to spend my last eight and a half years doing dumb shit. I overheard your conversation with Frank and Mike. I'm sorry but I don't think this is gonna work out between us."

"Not gonna work out?" He didn't give me a chance to answer. "Listen bae, you out of all people know what we have to do for survival. Right now, Antonio is the one who's feeding me and I have to do what he tells me. I promise you, once I get enough cheese, I'm out of this shit."

"That's what they all say, Chris. Once this, once that. Sometimes, 'this and that' never comes. I'm not asking you to change… Definitely not for me. All I am saying is that, I need to be on my own. Away from Cali. I need to enjoy life before I die."

"Katrina, I love you," he cried out. "This just seems like it is coming out of nowhere. Just the other day we were talking about living together, and now this? We've been together six months and I'm just now hearing that you're fed up."

"Chris, my brother has had me do some crazy shit the past few years. There's more to life than robbing and killing. The only way I will be able to see the other side of life is if I leave town for a while. If we are meant to be, then somehow everything will align itself and we'll be together again. For now, I have to go. Maybe, we'll see each other around. Something made us see each other at the mall that day and look what happened."

I had to leave. When I left, he was on the bed crying as if his world was about to end. I cried again too. I think I cried more because I left him with hope that we may end up together again. Truthfully, I didn't think I would ever see him again after that. I was done with Cali and all the bullshit that came with it. My next stop, Philadelphia.

Entry 11

New Beginnings

Buying a new car was the first thing I did when I got to Philadelphia. Even though I had made a lot of money these last few years, getting a new car was never on my mind.

I still kept my beat-up Corolla, though. I couldn't believe that it got me all the way to Philly without breaking down.

The new car was a Cadillac. A white one. I remember my ma used to drive one back in the day. This one was newer and nicer but it kinda reminded me of her. I missed her and wished that she was still alive.

I stayed at a hotel for the first couple of days. I had enough money saved up for an apartment but I needed to get a feel for the city. I stayed close to the area where me and Lawrence stayed when I came down there with him. I thought about calling him since I was there but then I decided not to. Lawrence was cool and all, but the more I thought about it, the more I realized that I needed to stay away from everyone that I was associated with back in

Cali. Plus, the way he left; all panicky, he had to be involved in something. It was best that I stayed to myself and keep it moving.

I even went to church. The hotel that I was staying at was an extended stay suite and the lady next door to me invited me to her church. That was my first time in church since I was a kid. For years, I had taught myself that God either wasn't real or didn't care about us.

Despite my beliefs, the sermon did touch my heart. The pastor spoke about starting over in life. That came at the right time because that was exactly what I was doing.

Los Angeles was on my mind from time to time but I was happy in Philadelphia. I was happy to truly be by myself.

■■■

I found a job at a liquor store in West Philadelphia and got an apartment nearby. My paychecks were about $850 every two weeks. My car note was $300 a month and the apartment cost $700. The neighborhood wasn't the best, but since I didn't fool with anybody over there, I was good. I worked the dayshift, and most nights, I just stayed home in my bed.

One night, I did decide to get out. I drove around the city taking in some of the sights. Philadelphia was a beautiful city. Especially at night with all the bridges and tall buildings in Center City.

I had never had an authentic cheesesteak so I went to the two popular ones in town and tried them both. Even though I couldn't finish, neither sandwich disappointed me.

After leaving there, I went to a casino which was about twenty minutes away. I had a lil cash on me and was just trying my luck. As soon as I walked in, smoke filled the air. It took me a minute to adjust to it. I grabbed me a drink and headed to the slots.

I put a $100 dollar bill in and in no time, I racked up some dough. I got a bonus round on one of the slots and came away with $800 dollars. I was happy with that and since I was already tipsy, I decided to call it a night. I wasn't really ready to go home, but I didn't want to spend the money that I just won either.

On my way out, I saw a woman standing near the front entrance. I was a good twenty feet away from her but she was staring at me and smiling. She slid in my path and slowly extended her arm out to stop me. It was gentle but came off as rude to me. I know she saw the look on my face.

"Hey, I saw you over there racking up them dollars, girl," she said to me.

She was a black woman, around my age or maybe a lil older. She probably was just being friendly, but I wasn't the type of chick to be smiling in another chick's face. I kept it real.

"And? You're watching me or something?" I frowned.

She put her hand on my shoulder. "Oh no," she laughed. "I was a couple seats down from you and I heard the jackpot sound going off. I won a few hundred on Poker so I'm about to call it a night."

I relaxed a bit. She did seem like a cool enough person to hold a conversation with. "Nice," I returned "So, what's your name?"

"Monique. And you?"

"Katrina."

"Come grab a drink with me before you go," she said to me. I walked with her to the bar and we sat down in the middle. I didn't plan on drinking anything else but her drink looked sweet and fruity, so I ordered what she had.

She turned her head to me after taking a sip. "You don't seem like a Philly girl; where you from?"

The music was starting to get louder so I had to raise my voice some so she could hear me. "How you know I'm not from here?"

"Well, no offense to the women here in Philly but I've been here for a few years and they don't breed them as beautiful as you are."

I didn't know if she was flirting or just complimenting me. She did seem like one of those girls who was into men and women. "Well, I'm from California. Compton to be exact."

She gently slapped my shoulder. "No, shit? Wow, I'm from Torrance. I moved up here with a good friend of mine."

We did a toast. "Alright, alright. I got me another Cali girl in the house!" I was a little excited.

"So, what you got going on the rest of the night?" she asked.

"Nothing, chile. I'm here by myself so I just go with the flow."

"You wanna come play some pool with me? There's a lil' hole in the wall off of Spruce that has a few tables.

A friend of mine owns the place so we can play and drink for free."

Hell, why not. It would be good to finally get out with someone. "Cool, I'm down," I replied.

I followed her there. There was literally no parking so we had to park a couple blocks down and walk to the pool hall. I had on flats and I laughed as she struggled with them heels on.

When we walked in, the place was kinda dead. I was surprised because we were in a busy area. Then again, it was kinda early still. We found an open pool table in the corner. When we settled at the table, she started acting a little nervous.

"Hey, you ok?" I questioned.

"Yeah, I'm good, girl. I'm gonna run to the restroom real quick."

She quickly left the table and went towards the front. I didn't think anything of it, though. I guess she just had to piss really bad. I waited for at least five to ten minutes and she didn't come back. Maybe she had to shit? Or maybe it was that time of month? I didn't see her leave out or anything so I just racked the balls up and played a game by myself.

Now, after another ten minutes passed, I did become concerned. I went to the restroom to check and see if she was there. Empty. I walked up to the bartender. "Hey, did you see the girl who I came in here with?"

"Oh, Monique? Yes, she said that she had to run. She may come back. She's a regular and lives right down the street."

"Well, she left her purse over here."

"Ok, you can bring it to me and I will give it to her."

How the fuck she gonna invite me then leave? Dumb bitch. I figured I would just finish my drink, hit a few more balls and then leave.

Once I got back to my table, I heard a lot of commotion coming from the front door. I looked and saw three men dragging someone inside. One of the men pulled out a gun and locked the front door.

"Whoa!" I yelled. "Let me get the hell out of here before y'all do whatever y'all about to do. I-ain' seen shit." I picked up my purse and headed for the door.

"Hold on, baby," one of the men said to me. "It's about to get real interesting in a minute."

This man was sitting down at a table so it surprised me when he said that to me. He wasn't anywhere near the men at the door. How da hell does he know that it's about to get interesting?

"Aye, where Blaze at?" I heard somebody yell.

Blaze? That name sounded familiar and then it hit me. Chris mentioned someone named Blaze who came here from Los Angeles. It would have to be one helluva coincidence if it was the same person. I was starting to feel like it was a set up. That bitch Monique brought me there for a reason. I didn't have my gun or any other weapons on me.

The small door behind the bar opened and someone walked out. His back was turned and he didn't look at anyone except the man they brought in.

"Kill his ass, Blaze," someone yelled. "He's the one who's been stealing from you."

When he got up to him, one of the men handed Blaze the gun. All I heard was pleading then a loud gunshot went off. The pleading and screams stopped.

Blaze put the gun in his pocket. He was about to walk back through the door but then he stopped. He turned his head directly towards me. He took his shades off.

"Welcome to my bar, Katrina," he stated. The voice sounded familiar. I had to adjust my eyes. Once I did, my mouth damn near dropped from my face. "Lawrence!" I gasped. "What the hell?"

I couldn't believe that it was him. Most importantly, I couldn't believe that I just witnessed him kill someone.

Entry 12

Double Life

Lawrence slowly took a few steps towards me. I couldn't lie, I was scared as hell. He was different. He wasn't the same corny ass dude from L.A.

Once he was close enough to me, he stopped and folded his arms while still staring at me. Almost everyone in the damn room was looking at me. The rest of them were carrying the dead man to the back of the building. "What is this Lawrence?" I had to break the ice since he wasn't saying anything.

"You tell me, Katrina. You never contacted me but all of sudden you show up in Philly? Did they send you?"

I raised my chin and kept a straight face. "Ain't nobody send me here, Lawrence. I came here because this was the only place that I've been to outside of L.A. I wasn't thinking about you nor any of those people that I left in Cali. To be honest, I had a lot going on in my life while I was with you. There's a lot about me that you don't know about."

"I know more than you think," he said with a grin.

Did that meant he knew I was robbing him blind? I just watched him shoot the shit out of someone and knew I could be next.

"See, I knew something was up with that girl, Monique. So, you spotted me at the casino and had her bring me here?"

"Let's go to the back and chat," he said to me. He walked away and I followed behind cautiously.

We went through the same door that he came out of and it led to a small office. There was a TV, a desk and small loveseat. Nothing fancy about it and it was a lot less attractive than his old club in L.A. "This is just one of three of my lounges," he said as he sat at the desk. "I own one off of Market Street and another in Jersey."

I sat down on the loveseat. He reached under his desk and pulled out a bottle of liquor. He poured it in a glass and took a sip. I just couldn't believe that he was acting this calm after killing someone. What happened to the Lawrence that I knew?

"So, you move to Philly and became a killer now?" I asked.

He chugged the rest of the liquor down his throat. He got up and stood in my face. He extended his hand and gently rubbed my face. "Katrina, I'm the same man that I was before. I can just move a little bit more with ease now. I have a bigger territory and less competition."

"Competition from what? Lawrence, I knew you as a club owner. Not a killer. What kind of things are you in?"

He nodded and smiled. "Well, Katrina, all I knew you as was a sweet, innocent and beautiful young lady. You did a good job fooling me, though."

I swallowed my spit. "What do you mean?"

"Don't worry, Katrina," he smiled. "I didn't bring you here to harm you. But best believe that I know everything that was happening in Cali. I know about the robberies and killings that you were committing almost every day. Just tell me no one sent you."

"Lawrence, didn't I just tell you that?" I said while staring at him. "I'm done with that shit."

He stared back at me. I didn't even blink. I kept looking at him until he finally looked away. "Well good. I was worried because you and I know the some of the same people."

"Like who?" I asked.

He sat down next to me on the love seat. I scooted over to give myself some room. The suspense was killing me. I wanted to know who we knew mutually.

"Katrina, the first time I saw you was at Club Obsession. I used to own that club. I knew something was up with you when you were sitting at that table by yourself. Then Ice comes and sit with you, and next thing you know, he ended up dead."

I figured that if he knew all of that, then he more than likely knew I killed him. I decided to come clean in hopes that he would do the same.

"First of all, yes, I did go there to rob him. When I got to the hotel, this nigga was in his boxers looking for pussy. He tried to rape me at gunpoint. My brother came in just in time and ate his ass up. I have no regrets about what happened, so if that's what this is about, then so be it."

He chuckled. "Calm down, sweetheart," he said to me. "I really didn't give a fuck about Ice. I'm just glad that you didn't try to kill my nephew, Tay."

"Wait, what? Your nephew?" I now grew concern. Tavious and I were kicking it for a while and we kinda just grew apart when I met Lawrence. Now that I think about it, the shit did seem like a plot. As soon as Lawrence and I started getting serious, Tay kinda took a step back.

"So, what was all this about?" I asked. "Why didn't you just kill me if you knew I killed your friend and possibly could've killed your nephew?"

"Kill you?" he laughed. "Katrina, you were doing everything that I wanted you to do. See, once I found out you were getting your hands dirty, I wanted you to do some things for me…. But, then I found out you knew some of the same people who I had beef with."

"I need names, Lawrence."

"Well, for starters, Chris and Slim. Once I knew you were associated with them, I didn't want to put you in a position to choose sides. They started closing in on me, so I had no choice but to flee"

I didn't know if he knew Slim was my brother or not. I just had to make sure he was convinced that I was clean and was in Philly on my own.

"You should've said something about it instead of just running out on me. Once I found out Chris was heavy in the streets, I left."

"Well, Trina, I wanted to, but like I said, you were involved with some dangerous men. Had I stayed, it would've been a war. I loved you too much to have something happen to you. I would've had no choice but to get at Antonio and all who worked for him.

"Antonio?" I then went back to thinking about the man who Chris was talking about. It all started to make sense to me. Antonio was the drug lord who took over Lawrence's club. "So, you're the Blaze they were talking about. Damn, so Antonio ran you out your clubs?"

"He set me up," Lawrence replied. "See, I started off as a legit club owner. I had a woman named Luciana who worked for me. She introduced me to Antonio. Once I got into the drug business, that's when I found out how deep he was in it. When he found out that I was moving a little weight, he sent some of his hitters to try to take over."

Once we got our past behind us, I relaxed some. I still didn't know exactly what he wanted with me, but we were having good conversation.

"So, why do they call you Blaze?" I asked him.

He pointed to a picture on the wall. "That's my pops right there. He gave me that name. He said that I was filled with fire and ambition. I had the power to set the whole world on fire."

Lawrence was finally showing me the *real* him. I had promised to stay away from the streets, but what Lawrence had going on seemed more like organized crime. All of the patrons in the front worked for him. He had shit set up nice.

*****

We left the lounge together and got into his Porsche. He wanted to show me the club that he owned by the river.

"So, you're the man around here, I see," I said while thinking about the man he had shot earlier.

He grinned and put his arm around me as he drove. This shit was blowing my mind. For once in my life I felt protected. Lawrence was on some gangsta shit now.

When we got to the club, he parked in valet. They greeted him by name and then came to open the car door for me. Lawrence came around and grabbed my hand as we walked into the club. Just before we sat down, he pulled me to the side.

"Katrina, since we know about our past, let's move forward with our future. I'm making serious money now… and I'm still that same nigga that you loved back then. I'm just hoping that I can get you to be by my side again. This time no secrets. I got a team that handles most of my dirty work. You and I can run these clubs and keep our hands clean. How does that sound to you?"

I don't know what was happening, but I was really feeling him. I couldn't control my emotions. "That sounds good, bae," I replied. Lawrence reached in and kissed me. "I got you," he said to me. Those words burned through my heart.

Sometimes good things come when you least expect it. I had a feeling that Lawrence and I were going to be good for a long time.

Entry 13

Money and Power

Lawrence surprised me with a trip to Atlantic City. He said that we needed a break from the normal routine. I recently started working for him as the club manager. I was responsible for collecting all the cash. He handled the illegal moneymaking side of things; the cocaine, weed and such. He wanted to keep my hands clean just in case something happened to him.

This time around, I was loyal to him. I had no reason to steal from him. He was treating me good and we were making a killing. From legit sales alone, we brought in at least ten to fifteen stacks a week. The pool hall was slow, and most of the money came from the lounge in Jersey. It wasn't no telling how much he was making from the crime side.

We took a limo ride to Atlantic City and stayed at a luxury hotel on the water. I had never seen a hotel so nice in my life. The room was stocked with a minibar and some refreshments. We had a full-sized kitchen, living room, dining room and two bedrooms. We also had a beautiful view of the ocean from a huge balcony.

When we got there, Lawrence went straight to the bed and fell asleep. He hadn't gotten any sleep the night before. I wasn't tired so I went outside and sat on the patio. I stayed out there for a minute, just admiring the breath-taking view. It wasn't quite *California style*, but it was good enough for the moment. The sun was setting and the glare was beautiful.

Lawrence woke up about an hour later. He came behind me and wrapped his arms around me. "You like it?" he asked.

"I love it. It's beautiful."

"Not as beautiful as you are," he said affectionately. He was still corny in a way, but it still made me blush.

From the balcony, we heard a knock at the door. I damn sure wasn't expecting anybody and he looked just as clueless as I did. Knowing we had money laid out on the bed, Lawrence quickly put it away and walked cautiously to the door. He had his pistol hidden behind his back just in case it was an unwanted visitor. He had me stay on the balcony as a precaution.

When he opened the door, he started laughing and talking to someone. I felt comfortable so I walked in to see who it was. It was room service. They rolled in a cart with several dishes of food on it. "I thought we were going to that steakhouse downstairs," I said to him. The food was looking good, but I wanted to go to the restaurant to show off my new dress.

"I'm sorry, bae. I thought that we were going to be tired so I ordered room service. We can eat at the restaurant tomorrow if you want."

I shrugged. It was okay. I could still put on that sexy ass dress the next day.

When we sat down to eat, he opened a dish that had some type of soup. It smelt really good. "What's that?" I asked while pointing at it.

"Oh, that's Lobster Bisque."

I twisted my face up. "Who you calling a bitch?"

He laughed. "Bisk," he pronounced. "I ain't that crazy to call you a bitch."

I was embarrassed for not knowing what it was but I did get a kick out of him correcting me. Once I tasted it, I smiled. It was good. For dessert, we had some type of butter cake. We also had a bottle of champagne. I was still the same way; it didn't take much to get me loose. I only had one glass.

After dinner, I was ready to get on those slots, but Lawrence said that he had something to talk to me about. One thing I figured out about him was he like to talk the most when he was drinking.

He sat on the edge of the bed and looked at me. "Listen, Trina. I brought you here to show you a good time, but I also brought you here because I need a favor. I need you to get back to what you used to do. Get your hands dirty just this one time for me."

My eyebrows rose. "Hands dirty? What do you want me to do?"

He got up and massaged my shoulders. I guess this was his way of sweet talking me or something. "I got three niggas in Philly who are causing me problems. One nigga is here tonight at this hotel. His name is Telvin. He be going round' the city acting like he sitting on big money and shit. I already peeped him out and heen' got shit. The other one is Dre'Mont aka Easy Dre. The third is Estevan. He's the distro for Telvin and Easy. I need Telvin dead, point blank period. He runs his mouth too much. He's also going around stealing my clients. As far Easy, I need him to stop buying from Estevan. I can set up a meeting with you two and you can try to get him to buy our product. If Easy buys from us, then we're good. That would automatically eliminate Estevan."

"Why can't you kill Telvin yourself? And if he's in Philly, why the fuck are we all the way out here trying to kill him? I'm sure we can take him out when we get back home."

"Telvin may run his mouth like a dumb ass, but when it comes to survival, he's really smart. He's smart enough to know not to get close to me or any other real niggas. That guy who I killed at the pool hall was working for him. His weakness is women. He lets his guard down too easy. You should be able to handle him quickly."

I was down with it. I hadn't killed anyone in a hot minute. Not that I was itching to kill, I just wasn't with people getting in the way of our paper.

Lawrence went on to explain that Telvin never had bodyguards around him. All he would have is whatever bitch he decided to bring.

This shit will be too easy.

Entry 14

Bye Bye Telvin

I slipped on a lil' body suit and a skirt. I headed downstairs. Lawrence knew that Telvin would be down there. He assured me that Telvin didn't know a thing. I didn't question it. I was just ready to eliminate problem number one.

I had a picture of him inside my purse. My pistol and knife were in there also. I knew I couldn't do anything inside the casino, so I had to think of a way to get his attention and make him want to leave the area with me.

I spotted him by the blackjack table. He was just as fat and ugly as he looked on the picture. The woman that he was with was just as ugly as him. The only highlight of her was her pretty ass shoes. Him, well he didn't have anything good going for him.

There were a few slot machines near them, so I walked over there. I made sure I walked in front of him so he could see me. He did just as I expected; he turned his head and followed me with his eyes. That body suit really brought my shape out. I then sat at the slot machine and put some money in.

A few seconds later, he whispered something in his girlfriend's ear. She smiled and walked out of the casino. He was still playing, but kept cutting his eyes at me. I ordered a drink and sipped on it. I glanced back at him, just to let him know that I saw him watching me.

Cameras were everywhere so I had to be careful. I didn't want to be seen walking out with him or even talking to him for a long period of time. To play it safe, I left the slots and walked over to the bar area that was across the room. Not long after, he followed me over there. I had a disgusted look on my face when I saw his dirty ass smile up close. He might've had money but he damn sure didn't take care of his teeth.

He sat a few stools down from me and ordered a shot of Henny. Once he got fueled up, he finally slid over and said something to me.

"You know, I've been watching you since you walked over by my table. My name is Telvin. How you doing?"

Oh my God. When his name, it was like a woof of shit hit my face. I scooted back a little. "I'm Katrina," I said while slightly fanning my face.

"You're from here?" he asked.

"Philly."

He got excited. "Ok, cool. I'm from Philly, too. I just came down here to chill for the weekend."

I glanced to my right and saw his girlfriend walk back into the casino. She went over to the blackjack table looking for him. He looked at her but tried to play it off.

"So, Katrina, are you doing anything else tonight? I gotta run real quick but I'll be back."

"Nah, not really. I'm mad at my boyfriend so I'm leaving his ass in the room all night. I wish I had somebody to hang out with."

His eyes widened, surprised by my statement. "Well, co-cool," he stuttered. "I'll be free in a few if you wanna hang out. I just gotta go collect my money and then head upstairs real quick."

I wrote down my number and gave it to him. He walked away. I was hoping that he would brush his teeth before he came back down.

I didn't want to wait around in the lobby for him. I went outside and walked around near the pier. It was dark but still lit in certain areas. I walked for a few minutes until I saw a small nightclub. It was around one o' clock in the morning and it was still jumpin'.

I sat on a bench across the street from the club. I could hear the music from where I was sitting. I just waited there until Telvin called. He called about thirty minutes later. "Hey, where are you?" he asked.

"Oh, I just went out for a lil' stroll," I replied. I got up and walked a couple more blocks then I told him to come pick me up. I wanted to make sure that no one was around when I got into his car.

He pulled up beside me. He didn't get out and open the car door or anything. He just yelled to tell me that the door was unlock. I rolled my eyes at him when I got in. He didn't see me do it, though. He was too busy looking down at his phone. He was probably texting his girlfriend or whoever she was.

I didn't smell shit so I guess he brushed his teeth. What I did smell was all that cheap ass cologne he sprayed. I had to roll down my window just a tad bit so I could breathe.

"What you wanna do?" he asked me.

I had to make up something. I wanted to ride far enough away from the touristy area so I could put a hole in his ass. "It doesn't matter," I replied. "We can just find a quiet place to chill and talk. My boyfriend done' lost his mind so it's whatever for me."

He grinned secretly, thinking I didn't see him. He then drove us around to a quiet area a few miles out. He pulled out a few mini bottles of liquor.

"You *won't* one of these?" he asked me. He was trying to say, "want," but his terrible accent pronounced it that way. I wasn't sure where he was from, but I don't think I ever met anyone who talked like him.

"No, thank you." I didn't know this guy but I hated his fat ass. He chugged three of them quickly and had the nerve to burp really loud when he got done.

"Excuse you?" I complained. He saw me roll my eyes that time.

"Oh, my bad, sweetheart. I think I drunk them too fast."

He cut the radio on. He was listening to some of the new school music and I couldn't understand anything that they were saying. I probably could have if the bass wasn't so damn loud. "Can you cut it down a little?" I asked. This nigga was annoying. I'm sure he was tired of my bitching. I had to calm down or he probably would kick me out his car before I had the chance to kill him.

After he cut the music down, he reclined his seat back, and started rubbing on his pants near his dick. He then looked at me. I saw him out of the corner of my eye and I kept my head straight.

"So, besides your lame ass boyfriend, are you having a good time down here?"

"Well, we actually just got here today," I said to him.

He waited like thirty seconds to say something else. "Cool."

"So, you brought me out here to fuck or what?" I asked.

His smile stretched as far as it could. "I mean... yeah," he replied. "If you down, I'm down."

I removed the straps off my shoulders, showing him my breasts. He reached over and played with them for a second. "Lean back and close your eyes," I said to him.

I don't think I had ever seen someone move that fast. He hurried up and pulled his pants down and let the seat all the way back. My purse was right next to me. I played with his dick with my left hand and took the gun out with my right.

He must've heard me messing with my purse because he opened his eyes. I already had the gun pointing at him by then.

He put his hands up. "What da fuck?" he said while shaking and trembling. "What do you want? You can have all this shit, please don't kill me."

I honestly got a kick out of his fear. Most of the time, I was killing niggas in desperate situations, but this time I had all the time in the world to watch him beg for his life.

"So, word on the street is that you're going around stealing clientele. You know that's a big no-no, right?"

Once he realized that it wasn't a random robbery but a hired kill, he slapped his forehead. "Look, I'm just doing what everyone else does. It's survival mode in these streets. Who sent you, anyway?"

"My man. Lawrence."

His shoulders relaxed and he shook his head. He must've known Lawrence killed his boy and he was about to be next.

My hesitation turned out to be costly. Suddenly, he grabbed my arm and tried to wrestle the gun away from me. We fought but his big ass overpowered me. He grabbed the gun and let off a shot, but it hit the windshield. I wasn't about to let him shoot me with my own gun, so I jumped on him and bit his arm. When he yanked away, the gun flew in the backseat.

"I'ma kill yo ass, bitch!" he shouted at me. He reached on the side of his door for something. I quickly reached in my purse and grabbed my knife. Just as he was turning around with his own gun, I reached in and drilled the knife into his neck. He held his hand on the wound, but the blood was coming out too quickly. After he lost consciousness, I took whatever money he had on him and ran out the car. I called Lawrence to come pick me up.

Entry 15

Easy

With Telvin out of the way, I had Easy up next. The plan for Easy wasn't to kill him; it was to gain him as a client. Lawrence knew that Easy had a bunch of territory so he was looking to do a deal with him where we would become his supplier. Lawrence had a good price for kilos.

Easy loved Chinese food so he picked a place in Chinatown. When I walked in the restaurant, he was already sitting at the table eating.

"That's rude of you," I smiled. I was a lil mad that he was already eating. I was kinda hungry.

"Listen ma, you were supposed to be here an hour ago. I got hungry. You wanna order something now?"

"Yeah," I said while looking at the menu. "Just get me some fried rice and an egg roll… on your tab."

"I got cha'."

After ordering, it was all eyes on him. Easy was one fine brother. He was about 6'2", dark chocolate and had a nice, athletic body. He also had one of them Philly beards. His dress code was on point. I watched his lips as he ate. It was kinda weird but everything was attractive about him. He even flirted with me.

"So, tell me, how do a woman as fine as you get into a profession like this?"

My eyebrows waggled a little as I blushed. "I didn't know that this profession came with looks. I just get the job done. Feel me?"

"Well shit, Lawrence is one lucky man. You fine and you out here handlin' shit? That's what's up."

The waitress brought my food and I started eating. I tried to be all cute and eat small bites even though I was hungry as hell. I was a little shy around him.

"Why do they call you Easy?" I blurted out. I wanted to take the focus off me eating.

He looked towards the ceiling. "Tell you the truth, I'on know. It kinda grew on me. My grandma used to say, *that's the easy one right there.* I think it came from me being quiet all the time. She loved when I came over her house. I always respected her. After that, my family started calling me Easy and it carried over to my friends."

We chatted for a little while longer, but I wanted to focus on business. I had some sample product with me and wanted him to test it out. First, I wanted to know about his current supplier.

"So, I heard that Estevan prices are through the roof," I said to him. "Lawrence is looking to save you some money and earn you a higher profit."

"What kinda prices he talking?"

Lawrence told me to get whatever I could out of him before suggesting prices. The plan was to offer a price at least twenty-five percent lower.

"It depends," I replied. "I think Lawrence is more interested in you joining forces with us. You can kick Estevan to the curb and we can get this money together."

"Man, I-ain' seen Estevan in ages. That nigga wasn't even running shit back then. He's from N-Y and only had a small area down here. A young nigga named Telvin used to work for him but he got popped a few weeks ago. Estevan probably ain't gonna come around here after that."

"What the hell?" I whispered to myself. "Estevan is not his supplier?" That changed everything. For one, word was out that Telvin was dead and for two, who that hell was his go-to if it wasn't Estevan. I was hoping he would tell me.

"Well, we wanted to do business with Telvin too," I lied. "It's a shame that they killed him."

"Man, fuck that fool," he roared. "Telvin was a lil bitch ass nigga who didn't know shit about the game. He let them niggas boost his head up thinking he was running shit. He got killed out in Atlantic City. Word on the street is that Toxic was out there that night and it coulda been him who did it."

"Who the hell is Toxic?"

He took a second to answer me. "My distro. That nigga run at least two-thirds of the city."

Hmm. *We may be on to something,* I thought to myself. I didn't know Toxic and I wasn't sure if Lawrence did or not. All I knew was that if he was the man, he was the one we really needed to get at.

"So, what is this Toxic dude charging you?"

He drew in a deep breath. "With Toxic, they're going for thirty-five or two for sixty."

"Pure?"

He snickered. "Shit, I wish."

I rubbed my hands together. "What if Lawrence could get you them for twenty?"

"Maaan, I would say he got a damn deal right there," he exclaimed. "But, that shit sounds suspect to be honest."

I didn't know if twenty was a legit number, but I said it anyway.

I had all the info I needed. We didn't even need to finish the deal. All we had to do was take down Toxic, and Easy would have no choice but to go through us.

"Well, I will get back to you. Let me reach out to Lawrence and see what we can do."

After finishing my food, I got ready to leave but he stopped me. "You said that you had a sample with you, right? Lemme see it. If the shit good, then we may can do business sooner than later."

"I'm not gonna show you here. We need a safe location. Just give me a day or two."

"That ain't how shit works, ma. Listen, I got a warehouse a few blocks from here. We can go there and I can test it. After that, you'll be on your way. No offense but I don't know Lawrence like that. I gotta see if the shit legit; otherwise I don't wanna entertain this shit. Feel me?"

"Okay." I knew it was good dope, so I agreed. He paid for my food, then we walked to our cars.

He drove a Range Rover. I followed him in my Benz. When we got there, it was one other car in the parking lot. As we got out and walked to the garage door, someone came out. "Sup Q," Easy said to him. They embraced. While they were talking, Q kept cutting his eyes at me. Finally he said something.

"This ya' new girl, Easy?"

"Man, I wish," he grinned while licking his lips. That's Lawrence's girl. She got something to show me."

"Lawrence? You're talking about Blaze?"

"Yep."

Q gave me a suspect look. He looked as if he didn't trust me. "You want me to wait on you?" he asked Easy.

Easy shook his head. "Nah, I'm good. Go head and head to the spot. After I leave here, I'ma take a shower and head that way too."

Q left but not without getting one last look at me. Maybe that was just his demeanor. I didn't know what it was but I was glad he was gone.

We walked through the garage and it was filled with BMWs, Mercedes and other nice rides. It was probably a chop shop. We walked all the way to the back to a small office. "You can wait right here, sweetheart," he said while pointing at the couch. He went to another area and came back with some kind of tool in his hand.

"You got the goods?"

"Oh, yeah." I quickly grabbed it out of my bag and handed it to him.

It took him a minute to check it. "Yeah, this some good shit," he smiled. "Tell Lawrence that we can definitely do some business together."

"Will do." As I got ready to leave, his phone rang. "What's up Q?" he answered. It was the same man earlier who was looking at me suspiciously.

I decided to leave while he was still on the phone. I already had the info that I needed and I didn't want to stick around to know what Q was telling him. I went out of his little office and started walking towards the garage door. Once I got to the other side, Easy appeared out of nowhere. He was holding a gun.

"So, you're a sneaky bitch, I see. You're trying to make me your next victim?"

I trembled. "What you mean?" I replied. He kept a safe distance from me. He turned the pistol to the side, still pointing it at me. "My boy Q just called me and said that he's seen you before. He then thought about it and said that he saw you at a casino in Atlantic City talking to Telvin... The same night he was killed."

"Huh? It wasn't me," I panicked. He probably could tell that I was lying.

"Bullshit. My nigga Q ain't gonna never forget a face. Now, I don't know what type of shit you and Lawrence on, but you need to call that nigga up right now."

"Ok, hold on." I opened my purse to act like I was searching for my phone, but was really searching for my gun. He was a good ten feet away from me. As soon as I got my hands around it, I dropped my purse on purpose. I got down and act like I was still searching. As soon as he took a step towards me, I pulled it out and shot at him before he had a chance to react. Two bullets hit him in the stomach.

He grimaced in pain. "Bitch you done fucked up."

I walked closer to him. "Nah, nigga. You done fucked up. You could've joined Lawrence and I and make some real cheese. Fuck you and Toxic."

I took a few steps back, aimed and put a few more in him.

I'm not the one to be fucked with.

Entry 16

Confrontation

Lawrence was mad. I mean big mad. I didn't initially tell him that I shot Easy. I didn't look at it as a big deal. Easy tried to accuse me of setting him up so I was in a kill or be killed situation. When Lawrence came back in the house, he ran up on me like he was about to hit me or something.

"Why the fuck did you kill him? You gonna have all his people after me! You gotta chill with this shit."

I wasn't about to let him yell at me. I stood up and got in his face. "First of all, you must've forgot who you're talking to. I ain't Monique or none of them other hoes. I'm Katrina. You can calm down with all that bullshit."

Lawrence knew that I was serious. "I'm sorry bae, I just want to know why you killed him? A war is probably gonna break out. Easy may have appeared to be a young quiet nigga but he had connections. Once word gets out that I had something to do with it, they gon' come looking for me."

"Well, let them come," I insisted. "You act like we ain't got people. You got all those men in your corner. All these guns in your house. Plus, you got a bad bitch like me. If they want war, let's give them war."

He paced back in forth nervously. He was starting to show his *bitch* side again. I didn't quite understand how he went from all cocky to acting like this over one person getting killed.

"Look Lawrence, he was going to kill me. He had some guy at the warehouse with him named Q. Q recognized me from the casino in Atlantic City. He told Easy that I was the last person seen with Telvin."

"Why yeen' pop Q too? Q is the main muthafucka who gonna be looking for me."

"Q wasn't there, Lawrence. He left and called him on the phone." I did raise my voice a little because I was tired of him acting paranoid.

"So, what do you think we should do now?"

"Look, you got me in this shit," I told him. "You should've known that there would be consequences. You got two options. You can leave town like you did L.A. or you can stand strong and take over this muthafucking city.

Nothing to be afraid of. You need to have that same energy that you had when you shot that man in your pool hall."

I hoped that the pep talk would help him. He was taking in what I was saying but I wasn't sure if it was enough to convince him.

"We took Telvin down, Easy down but I don't think we can take Estevan down. We need a whole army for his ass."

"No, we don't," I said to him. "Estevan ain't the problem. It's Toxic."

"Toxic? As in *Malcolm* Toxic?"

"I'on know him by his real name. I was hoping that you did. All I know is Easy told me that Toxic was his supplier."

That finally calmed Lawrence down. "Toxic is a low-key dude and ain't hard to find. I heard rumors about him and now I guess they're true. Muthafuckas used to say that he was the man behind all the operations, but I didn't think it was true because he was so chill. This nigga lives right here in the city. Him and his wife live in some condos. I say we sneak up on his ass and pop him."

"No, I will pop him," I corrected. "Let me do the honors. After this, there won't be any competition. We'll have the keys to the city.

Entry 17

Toxic

On my way to Toxic's condo, I got a phone call. I didn't recognize the number, but it was a Los Angeles area code. I was paranoid because I thought that it was my brother. He didn't have my number, but I didn't know who else would be calling me from the 213.

When I answered, I stayed silent until the person on the other end said something. "Hello? Trina, can you hear me?" It was my homegirl, Toya. "Hey girl!" I exclaimed. "How did you get my number?"

She smacked her teeth. "Girl, you forgot you called me the other day and left a voicemail?"

I did forget. And now wasn't a good time to talk to her but it did feel good hearing her voice. We hadn't spoken to each other since I left Cali so I wanted to catch up real quick.

"Girl, what's going on down there with y'all?" I asked.

"Chile' nothing. Kandy is still living with Slim. Plus, Slim and Chris beefing now."

I chuckled. "Yeah, I saw that coming. What they beefing for?"

"Some dude moved in across the street from Chris and he gave all of Slim routes to him. I think his name is Kevin or Calvin, I'on know. I don't be around there that much since Kareem not talking to them anymore."

I was almost to the condo so I had to cut our conversation short. "Listen girl, we'll catch up later, I promise. I gotta take care of some business. Love ya', boo."

"Love you too girl! Call me soon."

*****

Lawrence told me that Toxic comes home at 3 p.m. every day like clockwork. It was now 2:45 so I had time to get set up. His street was narrow and he always parked on the side of the road. I went down that street and just before the dead end, I saw an alley way. I backed in and shut the car off.

My shades were on and my gun was ready. A couple minutes past three, his car pulled up. He drove a 745

BMW. He stayed in the car for a few minutes. Someone was in there with him, but I couldn't see inside because the tint was too dark.

I was parked deep in the alley so he couldn't see my car. I was still in perfect position to get a good shot, though. I just patiently waited for him to get out. I got a text from Lawrence and as I was replying, I heard a car door shut. I looked up and he was out of the car. Before I could get the perfect aim, he walked over to the passenger side and opened the door. A woman got out, which was probably his wife. I didn't mind shooting both of them, but now had to get into a better position to do it.

A few seconds later, the woman opened the back door and a little girl got out. That was a wrap for me. There was no way I was gonna kill a little girl. I also wasn't gonna kill her parents in front of her. Since he was easy to get to this time, there would be another time in the future to take him out.

They started walking towards their building and I wanted to wait until they got out of sight before cranking my car up. As soon as they got out of my view, the little girl's head popped back into view and I saw a truck pull up behind them.

Toxic and his wife came back into view as well. They all walked to the truck and started talking to the driver. As they talked, the passenger got out and the little girl ran to him and hugged him. "Hey, Uncle Quentin!" she shouted.

I took my shades off to get a good look at him. I damn near pissed in my clothes. It was the dude, Q, from Easy's warehouse. I needed to get out of there ASAP. They were all outside talking to each other for a few minutes. I didn't want to crank my car up because I was sure they would hear it. Plus, I had to drive past them in order to leave the area.

A few more minutes passed, and they were still talking. I decided to try my luck and sneak out of the alley. As soon as I crank up my car, they all turned their heads towards me at the same time. Q walked towards my car and tried to adjust his eyes to see who I was. He recognized me because he stopped, quickly turned around and told Toxic's wife and kid to run inside the building. As soon as they did, he pulled his gun out and ran towards me.

"Get out the car, bitch," he yelled.

Once Toxic came over there, I knew I had to get out of there as quick as possible. Going straight ahead was my only option; even if I had to run them over.

I ducked down and threw the gear in drive. I was able to see a little bit and tried to run them over, but they got out of the way just in time. Bullets started flying and hitting my car. One went through my driver side window and probably missed me by inches because I could feel the wind from the bullet.

I almost got away but hit the corner too fast and crashed into a tree. My head slammed into the steering wheel. I almost blacked out, but my adrenaline kept me awake. I turned around and they were still coming. My car wouldn't start so I fired a few shots at them hoping it would buy me some time. Once they took cover, I got out and ran. There was no way I could outshoot both of them. Hell, I was surprised that I didn't get hit as I climbed out of the car. I saw a small park across the street. I ran through it and it led to another building. Kids were outside playing but those two dudes still gave chase.

On the other side of the building, there was a wooded area. I ran for at least half a mile. I stopped to catch my breath once I was sure that I didn't hear any footsteps behind me.

I called Lawrence. I needed him to either come get me or send someone. I kept trying but he didn't pick up. I tried calling Monique but she didn't pick up either. I had no choice but to wait it out.

No one called me back. I waited in those woods for at least two hours. The sun was starting to set. Since they hadn't found me yet, I figured they had given up.

When I got to the main road, I realized that I was close to Lawrence's pool hall. It was probably about five or six blocks away. I stayed on the sidewalk and power walked as fast as I could.

A Crown Vic drove past me very slowly. Once they got to the stop sign, the car door opened. I paused for a second and once I saw Q getting out, I took off running. Every time I looked back, he was gaining ground on me. I was now back in some wooded area. I thought that I was about to get away again, but I ran to an area that had a tall fence around it. As soon as I stopped, I heard Q approaching.

I had nowhere to run. I dropped my gun and turned around and faced him.

"It's over for you, bitch," he roared. "See, Toxic run these streets. It's hard to catch him slipping. You not only killed yourself, but Lawrence and his whole crew is going down too."

He aimed and squeezed the trigger. I closed my eyes and all I heard was a clicking sound. I opened them and he was looking down at the gun as if that was gonna magically make it shoot. I knew I had at least two more bullets and by him messing around, it gave me time. I aimed and squeezed the trigger. I didn't wait to see if he was dead, I just ran back to the main road and headed towards the pool hall.

By the time I reached it, it was dark. Normally, the music would be playing inside, but it was quiet. Monique's car was parked out front. She nor Lawrence still hadn't called me back so I was ready to go off on her once I got inside.

The front door was locked. That was unusual. I put my ear to the door and still didn't hear anything. The door and walls were thin so I should have at least heard people talking or the pool balls hitting one another. I tried calling Lawrence again, but still no answer. I had a key to the back door so I quietly crept to the back. I had a feeling that something was wrong. As soon as I hit the corner, I saw Mr. James sitting in his usual spot. The back light was normally on, but the only light was coming from the streetlight.

"Mr. James, where is everybody?" I asked. I waited on an answer and got nothing.

His body was slumped just a bit. My heart started racing. I walked over to him and tapped him on the shoulder and his body leaned forward even more. "Oh, shit!" I screamed. He was shot. Dead.

Shit. I had no more bullets but I pulled out my gun anyway. If someone was still in there, I wanted to at least scare them away. I slowly pushed the back door open and walked inside. The lights were off. I tiptoed to the switch and cut it on.

"What the fuck!" I screamed. Blood was everywhere and bodies were laid out across the floor. Not a soul was still alive, including Monique. The only thing that calmed me down was that I didn't find Lawrence amongst them. I was still worried, though. This wasn't a random hit. Somebody wanted them dead.

My first thought was that Toxic's crew got to them. I wanted to shoot my own damn self for not being able to kill him when I had the chance. This man was more powerful than I thought.

Lawrence best shooters, Big Keith and Ced were on the ground covered in blood. If a war was starting, it was already seeming like a loss for us.

I grabbed Monique's keys from the counter and got out as quick as possible.

Entry 18

The Last Ride

Lawrence finally called me. I was already inside of Monique's car headed home. "Oh, so now you wanna call me back? After I damn near got killed?" I was screaming at him.

"Meet me at the Jersey crib," he rushed. Don't stop for no one. I'll be outside waiting on you."

"What are we going to do?" I asked. "I just left the pool hall and everybody is dead."

"I know. Look, we'll figure it out later. Just get here."

His Jersey home was in Mount Laurel. I was about twenty minutes away. He kept calling me to check up on me. Just before I got to the Betsy Ross Bridge, traffic started building up. There was an accident a few cars in front of me. I didn't have time for that shit. I made a quick U-turn and went towards the Ben Franklin. Traffic was crazy over that way as well. I called Lawrence, but he didn't answer. I texted him and still didn't get a response.

Finally, I crossed over to Jersey and the traffic eased up. I did damn near a hundred the rest of the way. Once I got there, I saw Lawrence outside already. I let out an exhale of relief knowing that he was okay. I pulled up beside him and rolled the window down. "What the hell, Lawrence? I kept calling you but you ain't pick up," I complained.

He was shaking nervously. "Listen, I think my phone is tapped or something. Toxic called me. He knows where I stay. This guy got connections. I cut it off and left it upstairs. Are you ready?"

I exhaled. "Yeah."

"Okay, we're gonna take my car. Just wait here until I back it out."

As he walked towards the garage, a Chevy Suburban pulled up on the street. They stopped about fifty feet from the house. Lawrence didn't see them coming. No one got out, but I rolled my window down and yelled for Lawrence to hurry. As soon as I did, three masked men jumped out of the truck and ran towards him. "Lawrence, look out!" I yelled. He ducked behind the car and they exchanged bullets. If I had bullets in my gun, I coulda easily took them down because they weren't paying any attention to me.

Lawrence held his own. He took them all down one by one. I couldn't believe it. He then jogged back over to me. "Damn, I got their ass," he said while breathing heavily. "Now let's go."

He was still trying to get me to ride in his car, but it was filled with bullet holes. "Just get in here, Lawrence," I said to him. "We'll just have to drive this car."

He still stayed standing in front of the door. "I can't believe he killed all my people. I'ma have to get his ass," he cried.

"Lawrence, we can plot later. Let's get the hell out of here."

As soon as he finally was about to get in, a single gunshot went off. He groaned. The bullet hit his arm. I turned and looked at the SUV. Toxic was standing there holding a gun. He had been sitting in the truck the whole time and we didn't even know it.

Lawrence tried to get in the car, but Toxic started shooting again. He hit Lawrence several times. I screamed and panicked but there wasn't much as I could do. Toxic walked over to us, slowly and with confidence. I tried to pull Lawrence inside of the car, but he was too heavy. He was still alive but wounded so badly, that he couldn't move his legs.

"Just go," he cried.

"No, I'm not leaving you," I cried.

Toxic was now standing right in front of the car. He walked all the way to Lawrence and lifted him up by the collar of his shirt.

"So, you send a bitch to take me out?" he questioned. His eyes blazed with anger.

Lawrence was too weak to speak. I lowered my head so he could see my face. "Yep. And if I had bullets in this damn gun, I would finish the job."

I said that shit with confidence. It caught Toxic by surprise. He chuckled. He then held the gun up to Lawrence's head and shot him at point blank range. His body was halfway inside of my car. I knew he was dead but I grabbed him and comforted him anyway. I now knew how so many wives, girlfriends and mothers felt when I killed their love ones.

Toxic pushed me away and pulled Lawrence's body all the way out. He sat in the passenger seat. He was sitting in the blood and all. He held the gun up at me.

"Kill me," I ordered. I was shaking like hell but I didn't take my eyes off of him. I wanted him to look me in the face while he pulled the trigger.

He laughed. "Nah," he replied. "At least not right now. I mean, I should, though. You did just take out my nephew, Q and tried to kill me…. But, I think we're even now. I killed this bitch ass nigga."

I took a very deep breath and tilted my head back against the headrest. "Just do it." I was actually disappointed. With Lawrence dead, I felt it should be the end for me too.

"I admire your ambition," he said to me. "You're one tough ass bitch. You may feel like dying now but go live your life… somewhere else. I'ma give you a chance to leave town, and if I ever catch your ass here again, that's a wrap. That shit gonna be slow and painful for you. Now get the fuck out of here."

Toxic got out and walked back to his truck and drove off. After he left, I burst out in tears. I let Lawrence down and as a consequence, he lost his life. I will forever be grateful for the time I spent with him.

There was only one place I could go back to. Home.

Entry 19

Back home

During the journey, I may have stopped once or twice for rest. The rest of my stops were brief. Just to use the bathroom and grab a snack. I was able to go get my Cadillac before I left. I couldn't believe it cranked up because I hadn't driven it since Lawrence gave me the Mercedes.

As soon as I entered California, I stopped at one of the first exits. I needed time rest and plot my next move. I was damn near broke. Lawrence had all the money and I didn't have a chance to get shit. After buying gas and food, I only had about two hundred dollars left.

The hotel room was fifty a night. I booked two nights just so I would have enough money to get back to L.A.. I would have to find a way to get some money once I got back. But at that moment, all I wanted to do was rest.

It was a little after seven in the evening when I laid down. I was exhausted but couldn't sleep. It was too much on my mind. If I hadn't let my brother talk me into becoming a thief and a killer, none of this would've ever happened.

My thoughts were all over the place. Honestly, I couldn't blame him for everything. I made most of those choices on my own. Now I had to live with the consequences.

Entry 20

Toya

I called Toya up right after I left the hotel. She told me that she had her own place now and that I could crash with her for as long as I needed to.

I was grateful. I had no intentions on staying there long. Once I got my money stacked up, I would eventually get my own place.

Toya was already outside waiting on me when I pulled up. She ran to the car to the car and hugged me. "Hey, girl! I missed you sooo much!" She gripped me tight for at least ten seconds.

"I missed you too," I said to her, breathing heavily once she released her grip.

"So, what made you come back? Got tired of that cold ass Philly weather?"

"You crazy, girl," I laughed, but didn't answer her question. Toya didn't know much of what was going on in Philly and I wanted to keep it that way.

"Where's your bags?" she asked, opening the trunk. All I had was a few pair of jeans and shirts.

"That's all I got, girl. It's a long story, but I left everything right there in Philly"

"Well, we gonna have to get you some clothes then." Toya was a real one. She always had my back no matter what. She didn't ask any more questions. All she did was grab her keys and took me shopping. We went to a mall far away. I didn't want to run into anyone that I knew. She understood where I was coming from.

"So, you really done with them, huh?" she asked, referring to Chris and my brother.

"Listen Toya, if I could have, I would've stayed in Philly. I'm sure my brother is the same as he was before."

"He sure is," Toya agreed.

"And Chris… I was starting to fall in love with him but he didn't seem any better than my brother. He was involved in a lot of shit. I'm done with that."

"I feel ya, girl. Just remember that you can stay with me for as long as you need to."

I took her up on that offer. I found a job at a liquor store. I had worked at one briefly while in Philly and it was cool. This time was even better because the liquor store was in Long Beach. Far from everyone.

*****

A couple months later, I was able to talk to my old landlord and get my old place back since it was vacant. Toya was good to me for letting me stay with her, but I wanted to get my own space. I knew she didn't mind, but it's nothing like having your own.

Life is flowing well; I'm enjoying my second chance at life.

Entry 21

Nate

fter working a double shift at the liquor store, I was tired and ready to get in my bed. It was a Friday evening, but I didn't have any plans.

I had to get up early the next morning for work again. Besides talking to Toya, I had no social life. I didn't care. I wasn't ready to start back dating again, and I damn sho' didn't want any more female friends.

When I pulled up to my place, there was a blue, old school Impala blocking my parking spot. I honked the horn and yelled for them to move. Whoever was inside, paid me no mind and I was getting pissed. I could feel my adrenaline pumping. I honked again repeatedly. "Hey, you are in my spot!"

The driver's door opened. A big, tall, dark-skinned man got out. He walked towards my car. It took me a minute to recognize him but when I did, I slammed my fists on the steering wheel. It was Nate. Once he got to my car, he bent down and leaned against it. "Nate, what the hell are you doing here?" I roared.

He had that ugly ass grin on his face. "Damn, Trina. Things changed now. I can't have you calling me by my government name. Call me Slim like everybody else do."

"Well, I ain't everybody else. I'm your sister and I call you by your real name. Fuck all that other shit."

I smacked my teeth. I was so mad that he was at my house. I didn't know how he found me. Of course, I stayed there back in the day, but I wondered how he knew I was living there then. I rolled my window up, but all he did was came around to the passenger side. The door was unlocked and he had the nerves to open it and get in.

"What do you want, Nate?" I whined. "And how did you know to come here looking for me?"

"Henry saw you at the grocery store and followed you here the other night. He gave me the address."

"Henry? Chris's cousin? The one from Atlanta?"

"Yeah, he moved in with Chris for good now."

I shook my head. I really didn't care what else he had to say. "Look Nate, I know you didn't come here just to say hey. I've been gone for a good minute and I'm not the same as I was before. You're probably here to try to get me to do something for you, but I'm telling you now, I ain't robbing nobody and damn sho' ain't killing nobody. That part of me is done."

"Damn… So, Philly really changed you, ha?"

"Yep. Because Philly damned near killed me. Philly killed the man I was in love with. Now Nate get the hell out my car."

I did raise my voice a little and he wasn't used to that side of me. He threw his hands up and shook his head. "That's how you gon' treat ya big brother?" he cried. "Come on sis, we blood. Look at how you living, I know you wanna get paid at least one more time, right?"

"I don't want to do nothing but take my ass in the house, I'm 'tied." I was offended by the way he was talking about my house. In my opinion, I was living good. It wasn't the best looking house but it was perfect enough for me.

"Alright Trina. Before I let you go in the house, just listen to what I'm about to say."

"What, Nate?"

"I know a nigga who gonna be carrying five hundred thousand dollars cash tonight. He ain't bout shit. He's carrying it for Antonio. I'ma take that shit from him. Kandy rolling with me too for the lookout."

"Kandy? Y'all still together? I'm surprised she didn't leave you by now. She ain't as smart as I thought she was."

"Ahhh man, quit tripping, Trina. Kandy is smart. She's about to start school. I gotta get her out these streets."

I had to admit, the money part had me interested. He gave me a few more details and assured me that no one would get hurt. "Nate, if I do this, I want half of it. After that, I'm out. I'll take that money and buy this condo in Long Beach that I've been wanting to get."

He smacked his teeth. "Man, I can't give you half. I gotta pay Henry and Kandy, too."

"Henry? Why is he going?"

"Girl, Henry been putting in that work. He part of the crew now."

"Well, what about Chris? I heard you two were beefing. Y'all back cool now, I guess?"

I felt that Nate was hiding something because he paused for a second. "Ummm, hello?" I demanded.

He finally spoke. "Nah, that nigga stopped fooling with me after he accused me of taking a few dollars from him. Fuck that nigga."

I was tired and ready to go to bed. I wanted to know more about their beef but I told myself that it could wait. It did seem strange that Henry was working with Nate but not Chris. Who knows what he was up to.

"Alright, Nate—or should I say Slim, I need to lay down for a lil' bit. What time is this going down?"

"Meet me at the crib around nine or ten, and we're taking your car because they know mine."

"Whatever." I went in the house and took a nice, warm shower. All I could think about was how could I do this quickly, and disappear again. I'm not getting sucked back into this life.

Entry 22

Deadly Exchange

Nate told me that the guy's name was Kevin and that he drove a black Jaguar. We drove up and down the streets looking for him and once we hit Alameda, we saw his car parked near a house. I slowly drove past his car and stopped a few feet in front of them. Kandy was in the passenger's seat and Nate was ducked down in the back. "Nate, is that him?" I asked.

He rose slightly. "Yeah, that's him," he confirmed. "Now drive off before his ass get nervous and know something is up."

"Why can't we just run up on him now and take it? We're wasting time by doing all this other shit."

"Because, he probably don't have the money on him yet."

As I got ready to drive away, I saw Chris coming outside with two duffel bags in his hands. "Nate, what is

Chris doing out here? I thought you said that Henry was the one who was coming?"

"Shit!" Nate said as he looked up and saw Chris. "Just drive off before he figures out that we're out here."

I sped off. Once I got around the corner, I slammed on brakes and looked back a Nate. "You wanna tell me what the hell is going on?" I yelled. "Why didn't you want Chris to see us?"

Nate sat up in the seat. "Trina, just park in front of that house over there just in case they ride by this street. I need a minute to think this out."

"Think what out? Nate, what the hell are we about to do?"

My initial thought was that he was trying to rob Chris and didn't want to tell me. No matter how much money was involved, I wasn't going to do Chris like that. We were once in love and it would be slimy as hell for me to do him wrong.

"Look Trina, if I woulda told you that Chris was involved, then I knew you wouldn't be down for it. But trust me, we not gonna touch him. He ain't gonna be the one carrying the bags to the back. It's gonna be that other nigga you just saw in the Jag."

I didn't believe his ass. "So, why is Henry coming with us? Does he know the details?"

"Yes, Trina," he said with an attitude. "Look, Chris cut everybody off when he met this nigga. He got this nigga on a pedestal or some shit. All I want to do is get the money. Chris ain't gonna get hurt at all because he's gonna be sitting in the car. I sent a text to him from a burner acting like I was one of Antonio's men. I told him to send Kevin to the back to deliver the money. Henry's gonna have a mask on and take the shit from him when he walks through the alley. If he gives it up without a problem, then we good. But if he wanna act up, we'll have to put a hole in that muthafucka."

"Well, let's hope he gives it up," I said. "I am tired of seeing people get hurt, Nate."

Kandy looked out of the window and spotted Kevin's car. "There they go right there," she yelled.

Once they drove past, Nate was ready to execute the plan. "Alright, Trina, let's go back and holla at Henry."

Once we got to the house, Henry was already outside waiting. Nate rolled down the window. "You ready to get paid, cuz?"

Henry nodded. "Hell yeah, I'm ready."

Nate then got out and walked Henry to his car. I guess he wanted to make sure he understood the plan. I was still mad that Chris didn't have no idea of what was about to happen. Plus, Henry was shady as hell for setting up his own cousin. Once Nate came back to the car, he could see the frustration on my face.

"It ain't nothing to worry about, Trina. I promise. Chris won't even know you're there. I'ma have you wait in the car. Henry and Kandy are all the backup that I need."

"Well, let's just hope it goes like you say it will," I replied.

The warehouse was a straight shot down Alameda. We saw Kevin's car parked out front as we approached the building. When we got close enough, I saw Kevin in the driver's seat, but there was no sign of Chris. Nate leaned forward from the backseat and looked out the window. "FUCK!" he screamed. "Chris's ass must be in the back with the money."

I panicked. "What do we do now?"

Nate looked back at Kevin. "Turn your lights out," he rushed. "He looks like he's on the phone or something. Drive past him slowly and make a right when you get to the stop sign."

When we reached the back of the building, Henry's truck was already back there. Nate was pissed off because he told Henry not to leave the house before we did. Once we got closer to Henry, we saw a bloody knife in his hands. Nate rolled down his window. "Henry, what the fuck happened?"

Nate told me to park next to Henry's car and he got out and talked to him. I didn't see Chris anywhere.

Kandy got out with him. She looked terrified. She wasn't built for this life. I know she may have loved my brother, but I needed to talk to her about making some changes in her life. She was way too smart and talented to wind up in these situations. Nate was a real asshole for bringing her out there. All I could hope for was that everyone made it out alive. I still didn't have an answer as to whose blood was on Henry's knife, though.

I was at the end of the parking lot but could still see Nate, Henry and Kandy. There were two buildings and a narrow alley in between them. It was pitch black outside. The only light was from one of the office windows and a small street light at the end of the alley.

I saw Nate slamming his fist into the brick wall as he talked the Henry. I couldn't make out what he was saying, but based on his body language, something didn't go as planned. A few seconds later, Nate walked over by the dumpster and came back with a phone in his hand. It looked like he was texting someone. After he was done, I saw Henry put on a ski mask and go through the alley.

Nate pulled out his gun and waited at the end of the other building. Kandy was standing behind a tree between the alley and the building where Nate was. She was still trembling. I wanted to get out the car and take her gun away from her and make her sit in the car. I knew that if something went wrong, she wouldn't be able to handle it.

Nate saw how scared she was so he went over there and talked to her. He then walked her over to the other side of the dumpster and told her to wait there. As he was walking back to his spot, gunshots went off. They sounded like they were coming from the front side of the building. Nate took off running up front. Kandy gripped her gun. I didn't have a strap on me so all I could do was sit and be a look out just in case someone unwanted came through the alley.

Not even a minute later, someone did come through. He had long dreads and as I paid more attention, I realized that it was the Kevin guy. He looked frightened. He looked in every direction and when he turned around towards my car, his eyes stopped on me. I looked at him too. He was holding a gun. He walked towards me, slowly. Each step as he got closer, I got more nervous. I was about to run him over, but honestly, he didn't look like he wanted to shoot me. He was terrified himself.

I saw movement behind him and it was Kandy. Apparently, she had been trying to get my attention for a while because she was waving her arms. Kandy didn't see his facial expression so she thought that I was in danger. She raised her gun up and pointed it at Kevin and told him to put his down. She was trembling as she gave command. Nate came from around the corner again and yelled for Kandy to shoot him. I also heard him saying that Kevin shot Henry. Nate was wrong for underestimating him.

That split second was all that Kevin needed. Kandy took her eyes off him and Kevin reached in and grabbed her gun. She struggled and gave a good fight but Kevin was able to take it from her. She then reached back in and that was the mistake that cost her her life. The gun appeared to go off accidentally and it hit her in the chest. Nate had a bag in his hand and dropped it on the ground. He pulled his gun out and started shooting at Kevin. Kevin retreated but was shooting at him also.

Once Nate ran out of bullets, he had no choice but to retreat. He left that bag on the ground but there was another one near Henry's truck so he grabbed that one and jumped in the car with me. "Drive, Trina!" he shouted. "Get us the hell outta here." This was probably the first time I've seen Nate this terrified.

I sped off because I didn't know if Kevin was going to keep shooting, but as we drove away, I saw him standing over Kandy and appeared to be helping her.

"We can't just leave her, Nate?"

Nate's breathing slowed down once we were at a safe distance. "We ain't got a choice. She got shot with the gun I gave her. That was a .44. I'm sorry Katrina, but I know she's gone."

"So, what about Henry?"

"Shit, I underestimated Kevin. That muthafucka shot both of them."

Kevin wasn't just some random dude like Nate originally thought. I wanted to go back and kill him myself, but we heard police sirens from a distance.

"He shot them but at least I got one of the bags," he bragged.

That was the dumbest shit that I ever heard in my life. I slapped him on his arm. "Money? Nigga, you worrying about some fucking money and they're probably dead? And you never told me what happened to Chris? Is he dead too?"

Nate knew something happened to Chris. I believed that Nate knew before he even got in the car. The whole time we were out there, I didn't see Chris at all. For all I knew, that blood on Henry's knife could've been Chris's.

"Kevin shot him too," Nate finally said to me. It sounded like a lie. Kevin was sitting in the car when we arrived and it made no sense for him to kill Chris if they came there together. I didn't want to call Nate a lie to his face but I made it clear that it didn't sound right.

"So, who sent Kevin? Why would he shoot him?"

"I don't know, but we're gonna make him pay for this," he replied. "I need you to help me set him up. It can be like old times. You find him, flirt a lil bit and get him comfortable with you. After that, I will make my move. He never got a good look at your face, so he'll never see it coming."

The only *move* Nate was thinking about was getting that other bag of money. He wasn't worrying about no damn revenge. I hated him. I shoulda stayed my ass home.

I dropped him off and he was so caught up in his lies that he forgot to get his bag out the backseat. I was about to tell him about it, but then I thought about it. This muthafucka had me do a lot of shit throughout the years and he profited on me a lot. His ass owed me.

I pulled over on Imperial and looked through the bag. I counted more than two hundred stacks. This was my break. This was enough money to put a down payment on that condo that I wanted and be done with Nate for good. I had to come up with a plan to make sure he never saw me again.

Rest well, Kandy.

Entry 23

Long Beach

Not long after I took the money from Nate, I found a steal in Long Beach. It wasn't the building that I was originally looking at, but this one was much better anyway. It was only a couple of blocks from the water.

The seller was a man named Jeff who had moved down from New York. He purchased it for cash a few years back and was now moving back home. His asking price was $250,000 but I was able to negotiate with him. I told him that I was single and just looking to get something that I could own. He understood and brought the price down to $220,000. I had just over two hundred stacks but wasn't ready to throw it all into the purchase of a home. Jeff told me that if I could come up with at least thirty-five percent of the cash, he knew someone who could get me financed.

I went ahead and dropped an even, eighty grand on the down payment and my monthly mortgage worked out to be just under $1100. That was well within my range. I was paying around the same amount when I was renting. I settled in, and was happy to be away from everyone again.

One day, Toya hit me up and asked if I wanted to hang out. I had no problem with it but I told her to come to my neck of the woods. She agreed and we met at a popular jazz spot and got our grub on. Once we ate, we went out on the patio and talked.

"Girl, I heard Slim is mad at you," Toya spilled. "He going around telling people that you took his cut."

Toya didn't know all the details but she at least knew that it was involving money. "Girl, Nate can kiss my ass. He pimped me out of a lot throughout the years. Shit, we even."

"Yeah but do you think Long Beach is far enough away from him?"

I took a sip of my drink and I thought about what she asked me. "Umm, maybe not, but Nate don't come down this way. If he ain't in Compton or the southside, he's somewhere downtown. Plus, if he did venture off, he won't be hanging on this side of town. You know how hood he is."

Toya nodded. "Girl, I feel you. I'm looking to move out the hood one day too."

"You will, girl. Don't forget that I'm always here for you."

"I know you are," she smiled.

Toya was my main chick. We were a cut from the same cloth. She had a crazy ass family just like I did. I made sure to let her know that if she ever wanted to come stay with me, she could. She also knew not to tell her cousins where I stayed because it could possibly get into Nate's ear.

After we left the lounge, she came to my place and crashed. Police be tripping around here so I didn't want her to drive home tipsy.

"Damn girl, this place is nice," she said while looking at the outside of my condo. "How much this shit cost? Gotta be at least six, seven hundred stacks, right? Probably a damn million."

I laughed. She was a trip. "Nah girl, my unit cost me two hundred. A cute white man sold it to me for the low."

My unit was on the eighth floor. The ones above me were much more spacious and nicer and they were the ones that cost damn near a million. I never even been up to those levels. We do have a rooftop bar so I'ma have to check it out one day

"What are they building across the street?" Toya asked me as she pointed. She was nosey and talkative whenever she drank alcohol.

I looked over and saw a, "coming soon," sign. It looked like it was a restaurant or bar. "I'on know girl but I may try it when it opens. Looks like an upscale bar."

I went to the restroom. By the time I got out, Toya was knocked out on my couch. I grabbed a blanket out the closet and put it on her. I then went into my stash and pulled out ten stacks. I made sure that she was sleeping good and I put it inside of her purse. That girl had done a lot for me and she deserved it. Hell, she probably deserved more. She was going to be my homegirl to the death of me. We were going to find a way to get legit money together and all. Maybe open up a salon or some shit. I just hope I live long enough to live out my dreams.

Entry 24

Kevin (My Last Entry)

Three months into my new place, I was feeling good. I no longer felt the need to watch over my shoulder for anyone. I was in a peaceful state in my life. I couldn't change my past, so all I could do was embrace my future.

The bar that Toya asked me about finally opened and I wanted to try it out. I had went shopping earlier that day and picked out the sexiest dress I could find. I wasn't going there to meet anybody, but something just told me to go there as fly as I could.

I looked in the mirror before I left out and although I felt sexy, something was missing. I needed a piece of jewelry. I remembered the necklace that I got from Rodney and I put it on. Yeah, I still kept it through all those years—and once I put it on, my look was complete. I would probably never take it off again.

Once I got to the bar, I was amazed at how nice it was but shocked at how empty it was. There were maybe three or four people. At the end of the bar, I saw a man sitting down looking depressed. He had his phone in one hand and liquor in another. Normally, this would be my move to find out what type of money he was working with, but I was serious about me changing. I felt drawn to him in a weird way. It was as if my heart took over my mind and led me to him.

I stood behind him at first. I couldn't think of a way to greet myself. I didn't want to come off too strong or even too formal. All of a sudden, he turned around and looked at me. He must've smelled my strong perfume because I swear that I was quiet as I could be.

"Hi, is anyone sitting here?" I asked.

His demeanor changed quickly. I could see the glow in his eyes. "Nah, have a seat, sweetheart."

He pulled out the chair for me and I thanked him. He was kinda tall, baldheaded and had an almond brown skin tone. He seemed like a very respectful man. He did check me out, but it wasn't in a disrespectful way. He was just admiring my beauty, I guess. I for sure was admiring him.

"Hey, can I buy you a drink or something?" he asked. I wasn't in the mood to drink, but, what girl you know gonna turn down some free wine.

"Sure. I'll take a glass of Moscato," I said while smiling.

After ordering, he turned his body towards me. "So, are you from here?" he asked. I felt comfortable with his vibe so I gave him a little more than he asked for.

"Well, kind of," I explained. "I was born and raised here but then moved to Philly for a while. I recently came back about three months ago."

He nodded. "That's nice. I've never been to Philly, and I ain't from round here either. I'm a Florida boy."

I don't know what kept drawing me in to him. It felt like I knew him although I had never seen him before. At least I didn't think so. "How long have you been here?" I asked.

"About a year and a half."

"So, what made you leave Florida for Southern Cali? They're almost the same right?"

"Nah, way different," he replied. "I actually came here to go to recording school. I just recently opened my own studio."

"Good for you," I congratulated. "I'm hoping to get back to school one day myself."

"You live in this area?"

My answer stalled at first but I brushed it off. I pointed to the building across the street. "Yep, right there on the eighth floor."

He followed my finger with his eyes and then his eyes widened once he saw where I was pointing. "Wow, I live over there too. On the thirteenth floor."

That was a crazy coincidence. I was glad that our conversation was going well because with us living in the same building, I was sure we would see each other again someday. I was hoping that we could see each other often, though. His convo was dope and his vibe was just sucking me in.

I think we were well into our conversation before he asked for my name. I told him mine and his name was Kevin. I paused for a second. It sounded like a familiar name, but I couldn't think of anyone. Maybe he was the man of my dreams or something.

Toya texted me. I forgot she was coming over. I'm sure I looked rude by texting and being glued to my phone. She ended up calling me to tell me that she was there early. I hated that I had to leave, but I told him that I would see him soon. I wrote my number down for him.

As I walked out of the bar, I took a minute to reflect on my life. I only had a brief conversation with Kevin, but somehow had a good feel for him. If we started kicking it, he could probably play an important role in my future. Maybe he can keep me out of these streets… But I'm just babbling right now; who knows where we will go from here. I guess we'll find out once he calls me.

****

I've cheated death many times throughout my short life, and although I had a lot of good going for me, I still sensed that death was near. They say the good die young. I've done a lot of things that doesn't necessarily qualify me as a *good* person, but I know deep down inside, I have a good heart. One day, it may show. It's easy to see someone pain, and their reaction of anger, but if you take the time to know them, you will also see their sincerity. Their ambition. Their integrity. Their cry for someone to love them.

I pray that I am able to live long enough to make a change in someone's life. That will be enough for me. They say you reap what you sow, so for now on, I want to plant good deeds…And when it blooms, they won't be able to take a piece or a part out of my life to define me. You have to know all of me to understand me.

This is my story.

Katrina J.

THE END

Visit www.ronleath.com for new releases, updates and giveaways. Thank you for your support!

About the Author

Ron Leath was born in Jacksonville, FL and currently lives in Dallas, TX. An unashamed believer in God, a family man and a hard worker, Ron looks to inspire others with his writing. He has been married since 2008 and he and his wife are raising two beautiful children. His mission is to entertain readers with his creative fiction and also show the world that if you believe in yourself, you can accomplish anything.

Be sure to visit www.ronleath.com for updates and new releases!

9 781733 062923